LOVE AND LEGACY

THE TWELFTH NOVEL IN THE ROSEMONT SERIES

BARBARA HINSKE

ALSO BY BARBARA HINSKE

Available at Amazon in Print, Audio, and for Kindle

The Rosemont Series

Coming to Rosemont

Weaving the Strands

Uncovering Secrets

Drawing Close

Bringing Them Home

Shelving Doubts

Restoring What Was Lost

No Matter How Far

When Dreams There Be

Waves of Grace

Threads of Kindness

Love and Legacy

Novellas

The Night Train

The Christmas Club (adapted

for The Hallmark Channel, 2019)

Paws & Pastries

Sweets & Treats

Snowflakes, Cupcakes & Kittens

Tarts & Turnovers

Pies & Plans

Workout Wishes & Valentine Kisses

Wishes of Home

Wishful Tails

Back in the Pack

Novels in the Guiding Emily Series

Guiding Emily (adapted for The Hallmark Channel, 2023)

The Unexpected Path

Over Every Hurdle

Down the Aisle

From the Heart

Growing the Circle

Novels in the "Who's There?!" Collection

Deadly Parcel

Final Circuit

CONNECT WITH BARBARA HINSKE

Sign up for her newsletter at **BarbaraHinske.com**

Goodreads.com/BarbaraHinske

Facebook.com/BHinske

Instagram/barbarahinskeauthor

Pinterest.com/BarbaraHinske

BookBub/Barbara Hinske

Twitter(X)/Barbara Hinske

TikTok.com/BarbaraHinske

Search for **Barbara Hinske on YouTube**

bhinske@gmail.com

ISBN: 9781969752094

Library of Congress Control Number: 2025926549

Casa del Northern Publishing

Phoenix, Arizona

To my exceptional network of talented author buddies. You know who you are. Your warmth, kindness, and support inspire and encourage me every single day. I'm proud to be associated with you.

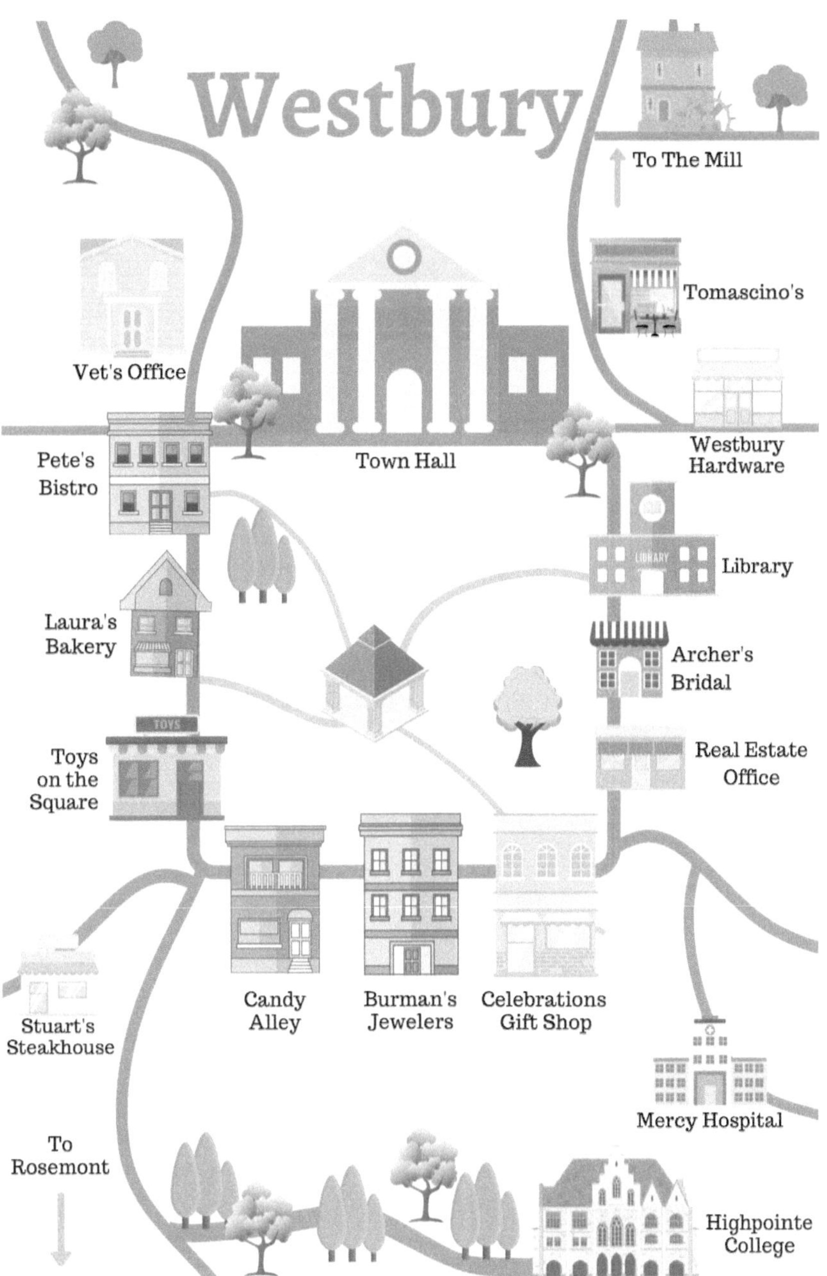
Westbury
To The Mill
Tomascino's
Vet's Office
Town Hall
Westbury Hardware
Pete's Bistro
Library
Laura's Bakery
Archer's Bridal
TOYS
Toys on the Square
Real Estate Office
Candy Alley
Burman's Jewelers
Celebrations Gift Shop
Stuart's Steakhouse
Mercy Hospital
To Rosemont
Highpointe College

CHAPTER 1

Sunday Sloan nestled into her husband's embrace. She and Josh Newlon had slept all night like spoons in a drawer, his right arm flung across her body, holding her close. The incoming storm had awakened her, but Josh slept through the rumbling thunder. His rhythmic breathing and the steady drum of rain on the roof combined to create the most comforting concerto.

A blinding bolt of lightning flashed across the walls and ceiling, causing her to flinch, waking Josh with a start. He tightened his hold as the booming roll of thunder swept overhead, then leaned toward her and brushed kisses along her neck. "You're awake."

Sunday nodded. "The storm started about twenty minutes ago. I can't believe it didn't wake you until just now."

"Sleeping soundly is one of the core strengths of your new husband. I like to think I excel at it."

"Good to know," she replied. "I'm a light sleeper. The least little thing wakes me. I tried to go back to sleep, but then I started worrying about Dan and Cara."

Josh rose onto one elbow, and she turned her head to look at him.

"Why are you worried about them? They're in good hands at Westbury Animal Hospital."

"I know that," she said, "but they're both so scared of storms. I hate to think of them being in kennels if the weather is as bad in Westbury as it is here."

"John Allen is their vet. If the weather is this bad there, I'm sure he'll give them something for anxiety."

"You really think so?" she asked.

"I do," he said. "But we can call if it'll make you feel better."

She nodded. "It would."

Josh peered around her at the bedside clock. "They won't be open for another hour." He smiled down at her. "Why don't I take your mind off things for now?" He turned her toward him and lowered his mouth to hers.

She slid her arms around his back and wrapped her legs around him. A sharp knock at the door interrupted them.

Sunday wriggled out of his embrace. "That'll be our breakfast," she said. "This resort is famous for its included breakfast in bed."

Josh drew in a ragged breath.

Sunday pulled the covers up around her and stared into his eyes. "We can't leave it on our doorstep in this storm."

"I guess you're right," Josh agreed with a hint of regret. He slipped out of bed, put on his pants, and went to the door. A chilled, wet wind swept inside when he opened it.

A trolley bearing their breakfast stood under the overhang of their porch. The freestanding English cottage was part of the elegant country inn that had once been a privately owned estate. Their breakfast tray sat on the trolley, protected by a clear plastic cover.

He grasped the handle and rolled the trolley inside, slamming the door shut against the elements.

"They're prepared for the weather here," he said. "This thing looks like a custom-made raincoat for the trolley, but I don't think it would have been a match for this storm for long." He smiled at her. "Your choice, m'lady—where shall we have breakfast?"

Sunday sat up and turned on the bedside lamp. "Other things distracted me when we got here last night," she said, arching a brow at him. "I didn't really look at the room. It's beyond charming—better than the pictures in the brochure." She pointed to the floor-to-ceiling stone fireplace. "Let's have our breakfast by the fire."

Josh rolled the trolley into place.

Sunday slipped into a silk robe and joined him.

Josh removed the dripping-wet plastic cover from the trolley and lit the gas fire.

Sunday moved two plates covered with silver domes onto the coffee table, which sat in front of a leather sofa facing the fireplace. She placed the carafe of orange juice and the basket of croissants next to them.

"Did you notice there's a two-person Jacuzzi tub?" he asked, pouring them each a cup of coffee from the silver pot.

"I did," she replied. "And there's a small dining table and chairs by that big window over there." She picked up the silverware wrapped in linen napkins and handed him his set. "I think there's a view of the valley beyond that window. It'd be a beautiful place to read and watch the storm."

"I'm sure it would," he said. "We're not going to be able to do any of the hiking we planned with this weather—at least not today. I think we'll have to find some way to entertain ourselves right here in this room." He broke off a large piece of an almond-pistachio croissant and popped it into his mouth.

Sunday speared a chunk of cantaloupe with her fork. "There's nothing I'd like better than a day alone with you," she said, swallowing the fruit and taking a sip of her coffee. "Did I see the basket of wedding cards in the back of your car?" she asked.

Josh nodded. "Frank collected the gifts that were brought to the ceremony and took them to his house until we get home. I brought the basket of cards in case you wanted to open them while we're here."

Sunday put down her fork and swept him into a hug. "I'd love to do that," she said. "Thank you so much for thinking of it."

He nodded. "I'll go get them as soon as we're done with breakfast."

"Let's eat up," Sunday said, casting him a sidelong glance.

She attacked her omelet with gusto. “I’ve got other plans for you right after breakfast.”

Josh grinned and pushed his plate away. “I’m finished,” he said, draining his juice glass.

“Me too,” Sunday said.

He swept her into his arms, and they melted onto the sofa.

CHAPTER 2

John Allen slouched in the doorway to the library and watched his wife scrolling through a screen on her laptop.

"It's not often that you get up before me," he said.

Maggie Martin tore her eyes from the screen and looked at him. "I couldn't sleep," she said. "I was eager to get into the excavation proposal Dr. Locke sent me yesterday evening."

"You said you'd look at that this afternoon," he replied.

Maggie sank back into her chair. "I know, but Fiona also sent the proposal to Anita Archer, and I'm sure she'll review it first thing. Anita's been most generous to the Highpointe geology department by allowing it to spearhead the excavation of the mastodon tusk in her basement. I promised they wouldn't interfere with her ongoing renovations and that the process wouldn't delay the opening of her vintage sewing machine museum. If Anita has questions, she'll call me—and I want to be prepared."

John smiled at his wife. "That sounds like you," he said. "How's it look so far?"

Maggie blew out a breath. "I guess it's okay. I'm no expert in archaeological digs, but I have questions about some of this." She tapped the screen of her laptop. "I'm going through the proposal again and making notes. I'll call Fiona as soon as I get to the office tomorrow."

"The college is on spring break this week. Will she be there?"

Maggie shrugged. "I'm not sure. The excavation starts this Wednesday, so I assume she will be."

"I thought you were going to take the week off," John said.

She gave him a rueful smile. "That had been my plan—and I'm still hoping to work less—but I need to make sure Anita is satisfied with everything first."

She ran her eyes over him. "You're dressed for work, not church."

"Juan called me from the animal hospital a few minutes ago," John said. "It's his Sunday to go in early to feed and check on the animals we're boarding. He said that some of them are unusually restless. It's drizzling now, but he checked the weather service app, and the storm that was predicted to pass north of Westbury has shifted south. It's supposed to be a real humdinger. I need to check on the animals we've boarded and medicate the ones that suffer from storm anxiety."

"That must be miserable for them," Maggie said. "I'm so glad that Roman, Eve, Blossom, and Buttercup don't have that problem. Did you already take care of Bubbles?"

"I'll do that before I leave," John said. "I was just about to pour myself a cup of coffee." He pointed to the mug on her desk. "Care for a refill?"

Maggie picked up her mug and held it out to him. "That would be terrific. I'm sorry the storm is headed our way after all. I guess that means our picnic in the country this afternoon isn't going to happen."

"I'm afraid not," John said.

"At least the weather was lovely for Sunday and Josh's wedding yesterday."

John took the mug and set it down. He came around the desk and pulled her to her feet and into his arms. "Every time we go to a wedding, I remember ours. Not a day goes by that I don't rejoice because you and I found each other."

Maggie nestled into his shoulder. "Sometimes later-in-life love is the best kind," she said. "I'd given up on the idea of finding my soulmate. And then—there you were."

John glanced at the terrier mix snoozing in her basket by the library fireplace. "Eve was the reason we met," he said. "Dogs have been the source of every good thing that's happened in my life."

Maggie chuckled. "I hadn't thought about that, but you're right."

A sudden gust of wind rattled the French doors in the library.

"Sounds like that storm is moving in," she said, leaning

back to kiss him. "You'd better get going. Don't bother refilling my coffee."

John retrieved both empty coffee cups and headed toward the kitchen. "Unless Bubbles has gone into hiding, I should be out of here in the next five minutes. We're boarding Dan and Cara, and I know they both need anxiety meds. I'm not sure about any of the other animals in our care, but it won't take me long. I'll be home in plenty of time for church."

"I'll be ready and waiting when you get here," she said, sinking into her chair and returning her attention to Fiona's proposal.

CHAPTER 3

Maggie and John shook hands with the minister and stepped into the narthex.

"Good heavens," Maggie said, pointing to the glass entry doors. "It's pouring out there. The storm really picked up during the hour we've been in the sanctuary."

"Sunday called while I was at the animal hospital to check on Cara and Dan," John replied. "She told me they've had the most terrible thunderstorms all morning—hail the size of golf balls. At least they haven't had tornadoes."

"That's good," Maggie said. "I can handle the rest, but I sure don't want to be struck by a tornado."

"Want me to bring the car around? With such a strong wind, I don't believe our umbrella will be of any use," John remarked. "There's no point in both of us getting soaked."

"Do you mind if we dash over to the coffee hour in Fellowship Hall? I saw Sam and Joan on the other side of the church, but I don't see them here. I'd like to talk to Sam, if they're over there."

"Fine by me," John said. He opened his jacket as they left the narthex. "Tuck your head under my arm, and my coat will act as your umbrella."

Maggie slipped her arm around his waist and leaned into him as they sprinted across the courtyard and into the Fellowship Hall.

John brushed the rain from his jacket while Maggie smoothed her disheveled hair. Only a handful of their fellow churchgoers had braved the elements to gather for coffee and conversation.

Maggie grinned and waved at the older couple standing off to one side, sipping coffee from Styrofoam cups.

"I was hoping I'd see you," she said, approaching them and exchanging hugs.

"I'm glad to see you, too," Sam said. "It saves me from calling you this afternoon."

"What's up?" she asked.

"Have you seen Fiona's excavation proposal?"

"I reviewed it this morning," Maggie said. "Something wrong?"

"Well, I'm not sure," Sam said. "I don't have any experience to evaluate her plans, but Anita is quite upset about them."

"Oh dear," Maggie said. "I was afraid of this. I have questions about the proposal, and, like you, I don't know how this should go. Did she tell you what concerns her?"

"She thought the crew doing the work would be much

smaller. Dr. Locke indicates there will be ten to twenty people there every day. That's a lot of people going in and out of that space."

"I was surprised by that, too," Maggie said.

"The rain today and the forecast through Thursday have Anita worried about the newly refinished floors."

"I'm sure they'll protect them," Maggie said.

"That's what I told her," Sam said. "She also commented that there's only one working bathroom in the building. She's asked me to complete the other one before the crew arrives. Jeff and I talked last night—we'll do our best, but we can't promise. Anita doesn't want to open the restroom in her bridal shop to the crew."

"Of course not," Maggie agreed. "She can't have mud tracked through her bridal salon. Can we rent a porta-potty if we need to?"

"That's what I suggested," Sam said.

"Anything else?" Maggie asked.

"I'm not sure," Sam said. "She was in such a state when she called me last night. You know how she gets when she's worked up."

Maggie nodded. "I'll contact Fiona first thing tomorrow morning. Fingers crossed, she hasn't left town for spring break. I'll talk to her about these concerns and let you know."

"Can I make a suggestion?" Joan asked.

"Of course," Maggie replied.

"After you've talked with Fiona, and are satisfied with her answers, set up a meeting between the three of you—Fiona,

Anita, and yourself. That way, Anita will be able to ask as many follow-up questions as she wants."

"That's a terrific idea," Maggie said.

"You don't need to be the middleman between those two," John added. "I'm sure everything's going to be absolutely fine. The excavation will come off without a hitch."

Sam cleared his throat. "After working with Anita on the renovations, I've learned she doesn't like feeling out of control of anything that's happening in her future museum. Everyone will be happier if Anita's calmed down."

Maggie raised her eyebrows and looked at John. "Oh my goodness. This sounds worse than I thought."

Sam patted her elbow. "Don't worry about it. You've got a solid plan in place to handle Anita."

"It's not until tomorrow—should I call her today?"

"I wouldn't," Sam advised. "Gordon's flying back to New York later this afternoon. She'll be leaving soon to take him to the airport. I'll text Anita to tell her I spoke with you and that you'll set up a meeting with Fiona. That should settle her down for a bit. If you call her, you'll just stir her up."

"Good advice," John said. "I'm sure driving to the airport in this storm will be exhausting. It's better to let her rest when she gets home."

"Speaking of which," Maggie said, "John and I need to get going. We're picking up lunch at Pete's and taking it to Susan and Aaron."

"That's nice," Joan said, joining the conversation. "She looked so beautiful at the wedding yesterday."

"Didn't she?" Maggie said, warming to the subject. "I'm

afraid that's why we're taking lunch to them—and why they weren't in church this morning. She called to tell me that her ankles are swollen this morning, and Aaron insisted she spend the day in bed with her feet up."

"That sounds serious. Is she okay?"

"I insisted on talking to Aaron, and he told me it's not uncommon for women at the end of their second trimester to have swollen ankles. There are a lot of benign causes—one of which is standing too much."

"Which she certainly did yesterday."

"That's what he said. He wants her to keep her feet elevated above heart level, and, if they're not better in the morning, she's going to see her obstetrician. He told me not to worry—that, as a doctor himself, he's proceeding with an abundance of caution."

"Makes perfect sense," John said. "And there's no reason for either of you" —he looked from Maggie to Joan—"to worry about this until we know there's something to be concerned about."

"All right, Dr. Allen." Joan turned to Maggie. "Will you let me know how she is tomorrow?"

"Absolutely," Maggie said. "What are you doing this afternoon?"

"My favorite thing in the entire world to do on a rainy day," Joan said. "I'll be in my kitchen baking. I don't know what ingredients I've got on hand, but I can't wait to get home and get started."

"That sounds like a heavenly way to spend the afternoon," Maggie said.

"When you're done at Susan's, why don't you stop by?" Joan asked. "Gloria Harper is coming over. It'd be fun to have the three of us in the kitchen."

"I agree. That'd be fun," Maggie said. "What are you going to do with everything you make?"

"I plan to drop most of it off at Frank and Loretta's," Joan said. "Any family with five kids can use food."

John chuckled. "You're right about that. What are you going to do while they're busy in the kitchen?" he asked Sam.

"I'll do *my* favorite thing on a rainy afternoon—take a nap," the older man replied.

John clapped Sam on the back. "I'm completely on board with that idea. It seems we all have firm plans for the rest of the day."

CHAPTER 4

Gordon Mortimer glanced out the passenger-side window. A highway marker flashed past—just a mile and a half to the airport exit. The windshield wipers clicked out a staccato rhythm on high speed.

"I'm surprised your flight wasn't delayed," Anita said, flipping on her turn signal and merging into the right-hand lane. "Hopefully, it'll be smooth."

"I don't think there's much chance of that," Gordon replied, glancing out the windshield at the stormy skies, "but it's okay. A bumpy flight doesn't bother me." He swiveled in his seat to look at her. "Are you sure you don't want me to reschedule my meetings and stay a few more days? I know how unsettled Fiona's proposal made you. I'd be happy to sit in on the meeting Maggie's setting up." He studied her profile for any clue to what she was thinking.

Anita glanced from the road and smiled. "You've got your

own life to live, Gordon. Your business is booming. The amount of time you've spent with me in Westbury is unbelievable. I wouldn't dream of imposing—especially since you said last night that you think I'm overreacting and have nothing to worry about."

"I didn't put it like that, sweetheart," he said. "I read the same proposal you did, and it didn't alarm me, is all."

"You didn't think I was being silly and emotional?"

"No, of course not. I'm sorry if I gave you that impression. Just because I'm not as worried as you are doesn't mean it's not important. I want to be there for you in ways that are actually helpful to you. If you'd like me with you tomorrow, turn around and head back to Westbury. I still have time to reschedule."

Anita pulled onto the exit ramp. "We've already aborted one of your trips to the airport," she said. "We're not doing that again—not for this. Your support means the world to me, Gordon. But I need to get through this on my own. I've been running a successful business my entire adult life. This is my issue to handle. I've gotten so used to relying on you, I think I've lost a bit of my edge. It's time I reclaimed it." She pulled to the curb at the terminal's departures level. "You don't need to be my knight in shining armor."

Gordon received her words like a spoonful of castor oil.

"If that's what you want, Anita," he said. "I never intended to intrude. Stitches in Time is your brainchild." He flung open the door and stepped to the rear of the SUV to retrieve his suitcase.

"Gordon, wait!" Anita called. She leaned across the center

console and called his name again, this time louder. He didn't respond.

Anita threw open the driver's side door and stepped into the blustery late afternoon. She ran around the car and intercepted him as he was lifting his suitcase onto the sidewalk.

"Were you going to leave without kissing me goodbye?" She reached for his elbow.

"No, of course not," he lied. "I was just getting my suitcase. I was going to come back to the car."

Anita arched an eyebrow. "Have we had our first real misunderstanding?" she asked. "I'm sorry if I sounded dismissive of everything you've done for me. I appreciate you so much, Gordon. You know that, don't you?" She rested her other hand on the lapel of his raincoat.

A security officer approached, blowing his whistle and making a rolling motion with his hand.

"I think he's telling us to wrap it up," Gordon said, nodding toward the officer. "I know, sweetheart. Everything's fine. Will you call me tomorrow to let me know how the meeting with Fiona goes?"

"Absolutely," Anita said. "And if I have any urgent questions during the meeting, can I text you?"

"Certainly," Gordon said. "I'm always here for you."

The officer reached them. "Let's go, folks—the drop-off lane is for drop-off only. Not long goodbyes."

Anita stood on her tiptoes and launched herself into Gordon's arms. He bent and brushed her mouth with a kiss.

"Drive safely getting home," he said.

"I will," she said. "Text me when you're home safe, okay?"

He nodded, grabbed his suitcase, and walked toward the double doors of the terminal.

Anita watched him go until the security officer pointed to her car. She groaned and slid in behind the wheel for the long drive home.

CHAPTER 5

Sunday pushed herself onto her elbows and brushed the hair from her face. “How long have you been sitting there?” she asked.

Josh turned away from the picture window and the endless green hills it framed. “About twenty minutes,” he replied. “I’ve been taking in the peace and serenity of this incredible view.”

“Why didn’t you wake me?”

“I didn’t have the heart. When was the last time you napped for an entire afternoon?”

“I’m not sure I’ve ever done that,” Sunday replied, swinging her legs over the edge of the bed and slipping her feet into the complimentary slippers provided by the inn. “It’s chilly in here,” she added, wrapping herself in the oversized waffle robe with the inn’s logo embroidered on the lapel.

"I'll relight the fire," he said.

She joined him at the window. "If we were back in Westbury, I'd find this weather dreary. But watching the banks of clouds roll across the horizon like this—it's absolutely beautiful. Dramatic, even."

"Everything I'm laying eyes on is stunning," he said, looking at her.

"Flattery will get you everywhere," she teased, settling into the chair opposite him.

"I'm counting on it." He smiled, got up to relight the fire, and returned to his seat. "What do you want to do? Shall we go into town? Perhaps we can find shops to explore—although they might close early on Sundays."

"As much as I love poking around boutiques, I don't feel like getting dressed or leaving. Staying in my robe the entire day feels like the ultimate luxury. Do you think anyone delivers food way out here?"

"That's what I wanted to hear," Josh responded. "I'd rather stay in, too." He picked up his phone. "I was searching online before you woke up. Looks like our options are pizza, Mexican food, or burgers from a fast-food chain. Not exactly fancy for a honeymoon."

"I can live without fancy if it means we get to stay put," Sunday said. "I'd be happy with pizza or Mexican. You choose."

"The pizza is from a chain, but the Mexican place is family-owned. I'd say we go with that."

"Decision made," she said. She stretched her arms above her head, laced her fingers, and flexed her feet. "Let's open wedding cards until we're hungry enough to order dinner," she said through a yawn.

"I thought you'd say that." Josh retrieved a wicker basket tied with a satin ribbon from the floor beside the door and set it on the table between them.

Sunday pulled out the first card. "It's from Susan and Aaron." She read the verse aloud, then pulled a gift card from the envelope. "Oh my gosh—this is so generous. It's for Celebrations," she added, handing him the gift card. "Susan says we should buy something memorable for our new home."

"That's really nice," he said.

Sunday went to her purse and retrieved a pen. She flipped the card over and wrote on the back. "I'll jot down the gifts so I can write appropriate thank-you notes. There are so many cards—I'm afraid I'd mix up who gave us what."

"That's my wife," Josh said with a grin. "Organized and on top of things."

She smirked and picked up another card. "This one's from Pam Olson and Steve Turner."

Josh narrowed his eyes. "Do we know them? The names sound familiar, but they weren't at the wedding."

"They're the couple Maggie and John met on their vacation in Linden Falls. They worked together to help the shelter dogs displaced by that horrible wildfire last fall."

"That's right!" Josh said, tapping his forehead. "They were at Maggie and John's for Thanksgiving. We talked with them for ages. I never expected to get a card from someone who didn't come to the wedding."

"Their note says they sent the card to Maggie and John

and asked them to give it to us." She flipped the card over. "There's a P.S. on the back. *'I know we only met once, but Steve and I really enjoyed our conversation. If you're ever in New England, we'd love to host you. We have a guest room with a private bath—you'd be very comfortable. Linden Falls is in one of the most beautiful areas of our region. Just ask Maggie and John! Our place would be the perfect home base as you explore. We hope you'll consider our offer. Wishing you the very best as you join your lives. Love, Pam + Steve.'* I'm surprised they'd offer that to people they've only met once," she said.

"Maggie mentioned that she and John stay in regular touch with them," he replied. "Maggie even said that, if she ever redecorates Rosemont, she wants to hire them for their design expertise. I guess Pam and Steve feel connected to Westbury. What do you think? Should we take them up on it?"

"I've always wanted to see New England in the fall," Sunday said wistfully. "But if we're serious about saving to buy a house, we probably won't be taking vacations for a while."

"That's true," Josh said. "Still, if we don't have to pay for lodging, New England becomes a lot more affordable."

"Let's consider it. Right now, I want to open more cards. At this pace, we'll be here until our first anniversary."

Josh chuckled and pulled out a card, reading it and taking charge of the enclosed gift card while Sunday logged the details. They continued that way for almost an hour.

"There's one last card," Sunday said. "It's wedged at the

bottom of the basket." She carefully pried it loose and handed it to him. "Will you do the honors?"

Josh slid his thumb under the flap and eased it open. "It's from Judy and Jeff," he said, handing her the card. "Looks like she wrote a novel."

Sunday smiled as she admired the iridescent cover, overlaid with delicate white doves done in quillwork. "This is the prettiest card," she commented, then started reading Judy's note to Josh.

As you know, I own a home on the opposite side of the street from the Olsson House. I grew up there. It's been in my family for decades. It's not as large or grand as the other houses on the street, but it has always been my little slice of heaven. I thought I'd live there forever—until I took leave of my senses and bought the Olsson House at a tax foreclosure auction.

I felt impulsive at the time—like I'd lost my mind—and maybe I had. But it turned out to be the best decision of my life. Buying that house led me to Jeff Carson, and the happy married life we're living.

I realized I'd one day sell my old home, but I also knew it had to go to someone who would love it like I do. No one fit the bill—until you and Josh came along.

Jeff and I saw you admiring the house on New Year's Eve. I didn't realize it was you at the time, but I remarked to Jeff that I hoped that couple—standing in the dark, studying my house—would be the next owners. Now here you are.

If you're sincere in your desire to own my home, I would be honored to make that happen. I've already talked to Tim Knudsen. He said there are several ways to do this before you have all the funds for a traditional purchase—lease-option, seller carryback, etc. I won't go into all that now.

Reach out to Tim if you're interested. If you're not, no worries. Please don't feel pressured. It just means someone else is meant to have the house.

But if you want it to be yours, let's do it!

With love,

Judy and Jeff

Sunday pressed the card to her chest, eyes shining with tears. "I can't believe this," she whispered.

Josh took the card and skimmed it. "They're going to make it possible for us to own that house," he said, shaking his head in disbelief.

"Do you want to?" Sunday asked. "I've always loved it—but this has to be something we both agree on." Her tone was calm, but her eyes were pleading.

"We haven't seen the inside," he said. "We need to do that before we decide."

"Of course. And it may turn out we don't like it or can't afford it. But we should find out."

"I agree. The sooner the better."

"If this works out, maybe we could move in this summer." She sat up straighter, glancing around. "Is there any paper in here? I want to start a list."

"I think the to-do list can wait," Josh said, reaching across the table to cover her hands with his. "I don't want either of us getting too invested if it doesn't pan out."

She met his gaze.

"It's too late, isn't it?" he asked. "You're already fully

committed, and you'll be devastated if we can't get into that house."

"I'm afraid so," she whispered.

"Well, there's only one thing to do."

She arched an eyebrow. "What?"

"Let's call Tim Knudsen and set up an appointment as soon as possible."

"We're booked here for two more nights," Sunday said.

"It's supposed to rain the whole time," Josh replied. "We can't picnic or hike like we planned. If Tim is available, I say we go back to Westbury. I want to know about this house."

Sunday clasped her hands to her chest. "Thank you for being willing to do that. I was hoping you'd suggest that, but I didn't want to ask to leave our honeymoon early. That seemed like bad karma."

"I know you well enough, Sunday Sloan, to recognize when you've got the bit between your teeth."

Sunday laughed. "I won't deny it. I can't wait to step inside our new home."

CHAPTER 6

Maggie leaned over the tray of sugar cookies on the counter in front of her. She'd chosen twelve cookies shaped like the face of a flower. She frosted the petals of the cookies in vibrant shades of lavender, pink, turquoise, orange, apple green, and yellow—two cookies in each color. Round discs in complementary shades represented the pistils. Still, something felt unfinished, so she meticulously encircled each pistil with a ring of tiny white icing dots.

Joan removed the final cookie sheet from the oven and set it on the counter to cool. "That's the last of them," she said. "I made a double batch since both of you were here to help decorate. We've got a lot of cookies." She walked to the kitchen island, where Maggie and Gloria were creating their masterpieces in icing.

"Gloria Harper," Joan said admiringly, "you are a culinary

genius. If you were on that British baking show, they'd say your piping work is extraordinary."

Gloria peered over the top of her half-moon glasses. "That's what comes of more than eighty years of experience decorating cookies," she said. "I learned from my grandmother when I was a child, and have always loved doing this."

Maggie placed the final white dot on her last cookie, then set down her icing bag. She turned to admire Gloria's tray. "Your cookies look exactly like dahlias," she said. "I don't know how you manipulate the icing to make each petal look so realistic. They're stunning."

Gloria flushed with pleasure. "As I said—eighty-plus years of practice."

"They're too pretty to eat," Joan said, shaking her head.

"That's ridiculous," Gloria replied, chuckling. "The whole point of cookies is to eat them." She looked at Maggie's tray. "Yours are stunning, too."

Maggie shrugged. "They're basic compared to yours."

"Your style is different from mine," Gloria said. "Those are vibrant and happy cookies. The way you shaped the petals in icing is lovely. Those white dots make the whole thing pop."

Maggie protested, but Joan cut in. "Gloria's right, Maggie. They're charming. They'll bring a smile to everyone who sees them."

"People will *definitely* smile when they taste your recipe, Joan," Maggie said. She pointed to a paper napkin with a half-eaten cookie on it. "They're delicious. This is my third one. I've been nibbling at broken cookies while I work—I hope that's okay."

"Of course it is," Joan said. "That's the rule. If a cookie breaks, you get to eat it."

"I'm doing the same," Gloria added, pointing to a cookie she had been sampling. "Is this really your first time decorating sugar cookies?"

"It's my first time using a pastry bag and tip," Maggie said. "I've slapped on icing with a knife—I had no idea using an icing bag was so much fun. I really enjoyed myself."

"Gloria and I do this every couple of months," Joan said. "We'll invite you to join us next time. I know your schedule's terribly busy, but I think it will do you good to spend an afternoon now and then on a creative outlet."

Maggie reached for her half-eaten cookie. "I'd love that," she said. "Spending a tranquil afternoon in the kitchen with both of you—that's the real gift."

"Then it's settled," Joan said. "There's always something going on in town to celebrate with decorated sugar cookies."

Maggie laughed. "Doesn't Laura's Bakery specialize in those? We don't want to step on her toes."

"Of course not," Joan said. "Her work is way beyond what we do here. Did you see those sewing machine cookies she made for the opening of Anita's exhibit at the Highpointe College Library?"

"I did," Maggie said. "They were works of art."

"We donate cookies for smaller occasions, where people don't have the budget to buy cookies," Joan said.

"I like the sound of that," Maggie agreed.

"While this last batch cools, I suggest you each pick out a couple to take home. I know your husbands will expect them."

Gloria laughed. "You've got that right. Glenn greets me at the door when I come home from baking with you like he's a dog waiting for his master. If Glenn had a tail, it would be wagging at warp speed."

Maggie chuckled. "That's a good description," she said, accepting the paper plate Joan held out. She placed two of her cookies on it.

Gloria leaned over and added two of her dahlia cookies. "Let's take home two cookies from each of us," she suggested.

"Wouldn't say no to that," Maggie said.

Gloria selected her cookies, and Joan placed four more from the latest batch in front of each of them.

"I'll take a turn decorating now," Joan said. "Since all the batter's baked, I have time. I'm going to make mine look like daisies—white petals outlined in pink, with centers made of tiny yellow dots."

The three women bent to their tasks, and, before long, they stood back and admired their handiwork.

"This *is* a lot of cookies," Joan said, doing a quick count. "Even after the broken ones we ate and the ones we're keeping for our husbands, we've still got ten dozen. That's a lot to take to Frank and Loretta."

"I've got a suggestion," Gloria said. "We'll send some home with Maggie for John to take to Westbury Animal Hospital tomorrow."

"That's so thoughtful," Maggie said. "I'm sure the staff will adore the treat."

"I agree," Joan said. "That's what we'll do. I should've frozen some of the dough, but we were on a roll and having such a good time, I just kept baking." She gestured at the sea of cookies. "I feel like a home gardener with a bumper crop of zucchini who the neighbors eventually avoid."

Gloria and Maggie laughed.

"These sugar cookies will be more welcome than zucchini," Gloria said, "but I get your meaning."

"Let's get these packed up," Joan said, pointing to a stack of cardboard bakery boxes at the end of the counter. "I bought those online—they're so handy. With wax paper between layers, we can fit two dozen cookies per box."

The three women set to work, carefully packing each masterpiece of flour, butter, and sugar. They were taping the last boxes shut when Sam shuffled into the kitchen.

His eyes swept the room, and his expression fell like a soufflé after the oven door has been slammed. "I guess I'm too late," he grumbled.

Joan rolled her eyes and pointed to a paper plate in the corner of the counter.

His smile broke like the sun through storm clouds.

"You know your wife better than that, Sam Torres," Maggie teased. "Of course she saved some for you. I'll help clean up and then get out of your hair."

"It's going to be dark soon," Sam said. "Maggie, you'd better get home and wake that husband of yours—if he's still asleep in front of the TV."

Maggie laughed. "There's some truth in that."

"I called Glenn before I came in to check on you," Sam said to Gloria. "I offered to give you a ride home, so he doesn't have to come out in this weather. Joan and I will drop you off, then swing by Frank and Loretta's with the cookies. I napped while you worked hard this afternoon. I'll clean up the kitchen when we get home."

"That's awfully nice of you," Gloria said.

"It's the least I can do," Sam replied. "Now, ladies—if you're finished—grab your cookies and your coats, and let's hit the road."

CHAPTER 7

"Mrs. Torres!" The barking of the three dogs pacing behind her at the front door nearly drowned out Marissa Nash's voice. She turned to Sally, Snowball, and Daisy, commanding them to be quiet and sit. The obedient Daisy snapped her mouth shut and dropped to the floor. Sally, Frank Haynes' geriatric border collie, did as she was told, though it took her a little longer. The high-spirited miniature schnauzer, Snowball, was the last to fall in line.

Marissa opened the door. "Would you like to come in?"

"I'm dropping off these cookies," Joan said. "Gloria, Maggie, and I spent the entire afternoon baking. I won't intrude—I just wanted to leave these for you."

"Here, let me take them," Marissa said, reaching for the three bakery boxes. "Mom's in the kitchen feeding the twins and making dinner. She'll want to see you. Will you come say hi?"

"Of course," Joan said with a smile.

Marissa led the way to the kitchen, with Joan close behind.

Loretta Nash was bent over a highchair, mopping up orange-colored puréed vegetables that covered the tray table and were dripping onto the floor. The oven timer was beeping, and the microwave was chiming and flashing the word END on the electronic readout.

Marissa looked for an open spot on the counter to place the bakery boxes.

Bonnie, in her highchair, kicked her feet and pointed behind Loretta.

Loretta straightened and turned, brushing a loose strand of hair from her forehead and smearing orange goo across it. "Joan," she cried in a weary voice. "I'm sorry, was I—were we—expecting you?"

"No," Joan said. "I'm dropping in unannounced. Forgive me."

"Mrs. Torres brought us cookies," Marissa said, still holding the boxes. "I'm looking for a place to set them."

Loretta glanced around. "It's chaos in here, I'm afraid. Frank was supposed to be home all day to help with the twins. I had a really nice beef bourguignon planned for dinner, but then he and Sean got called to Forever Friends for an emergency a couple of hours ago."

She cleared a space on the kitchen island and gestured for Marissa to put the boxes down. "Frank promised me he wouldn't be long—forty-five minutes at most." She looked at the clock above the stove. "That was two hours and fifteen minutes ago, and they're still not home." Her voice rose in pitch. She walked to the oven, silenced the timer, and reduced the temperature to 200 degrees. "I guess I'll keep dinner warm—again."

"You've got your hands full, dear," Joan said gently.

"Where are my manners? Can I get you something to drink?"

"No. As I said, I don't intend to stay. I only came to drop these off."

"That's incredibly kind of you," Loretta said. "Especially driving them over in this weather. I appreciate it. At least our dessert will be lovely." She lifted the lid of the top bakery box and gasped. "These are absolutely beautiful. They're works of art! You made all these? Three boxes of them?"

"I had help," Joan admitted. "Maggie and Gloria were with me. Gloria did the ones that look like dahlias. Maggie decorated the brightly colored ones, and I made the daisies."

"They're all gorgeous," Loretta said.

Marissa hovered behind her, eyeing the cookies.

"What do you think?" she asked her daughter. "Should we each try one now?"

"You mean before supper?" Marissa asked.

"I haven't eaten since breakfast, and I'm starving," Loretta said. "Besides—after the afternoon we've had, I think we deserve a treat." She turned to Joan. "Do you mind if we dig in?"

"Of course not," Joan said warmly. "We made them for you. And, for the record, I agree—you deserve a treat."

Loretta turned to her daughter. "Grab one for yourself. And take a cookie to Nicole, too. Poor thing has been in bed all day with a nasty cold."

"Then I think a delicious sugar cookie is exactly what she needs," Joan agreed.

Marissa selected two of the brightly colored cookies Maggie had decorated. "These are happy," she said. "Nicole will love them." She headed down the hallway toward her younger sister's bedroom.

"I think you're having a terrible, horrible, no good, very bad day," Joan said, referencing the children's book. "But how's it going in general? You missed the last book club meeting."

"Things have been better," Loretta admitted. She selected a cookie and took a bite. "Frank has been home more—until the last month. He's been working late, finalizing the construction plans for Forever Guides."

"Building a guide dog training facility is a huge undertaking," Joan said.

"The groundbreaking ceremony is a week from Monday, so he's putting in long hours now. But once construction starts, he promised me he'll be back to normal."

"The fact that you're managing the house and the kids and keeping the family going allows Frank to concentrate on Forever Guides," Joan said. "I want you to know I see that. You're contributing, too. I appreciate everything you're doing to make this happen."

Loretta's shoulders sagged a little less. "Thank you for saying that. Sometimes … I feel invisible." She took a second bite of her cookie.

"You're not," Joan said firmly. "Lots of people—the entire book club—know how hard you work to support Frank's charities."

"These are especially good," Loretta said, licking icing from her fingers. "I'd love your recipe. Marissa, Nicole, and I plan to bake cookies for the groundbreaking. I bought these adorable dog-shaped cookie cutters." She groaned. "I must've been hallucinating when I suggested the idea to the girls. I don't know when we'll find the time."

Joan tilted her head. "I've got a suggestion. Why don't the three of you come to my house on Sunday to bake them in my kitchen? I'm sure Gloria will join us, and, if Maggie's free, I know she'd love to help. Make sure Frank's home to watch the twins—or get a babysitter—so you can get out of the house and bake without interruption. With two, maybe three extra pairs of hands, we'll finish in no time. Plus, it'll be so much more fun."

Loretta looked into Joan's eyes. "Are you serious?"

"Absolutely," Joan said. "In fact, I insist. It'll allow Gloria and me to feel like we're contributing, too."

Relief washed over Loretta like butter on hot toast. "You're on," she said.

"Let's start at noon," Joan suggested. "That'll give me time to get home from church and change my clothes. I'll have lunch ready for us, and then we'll get busy baking."

Loretta grinned. "I'd give you the biggest hug, but I've got baby food all over me. I don't want to get you dirty."

Joan walked over and pecked her on the cheek. "See you next Sunday. Bring those cookie cutters—I'll take care of the rest."

CHAPTER 8

Alistair

Maggie was in the butler's pantry! She never went in there unless we were hosting a large event, and I'd heard nothing about an upcoming party. Even though I had been dead for decades, I knew when we were entertaining at Rosemont.

She had told John she'd be working from home today. He pointed out she shouldn't work, given it was her spring break. Maggie responded she was going to write her commencement address, and that Fiona and Anita were coming over mid-afternoon for a meeting.

I knew and liked Anita—she and Gordon both appreciated the beauty of old things. This Fiona was a mystery to me. I didn't think I'd ever seen her.

I trailed into the butler's pantry after Maggie. It was by far my favorite room in the house when I was alive. I had spent many happy hours there. Now that I was on the other side, I was comfortable in my attic, but I still enjoyed spending time in my former domain.

"I've invited Dr. Fiona Locke, the head of the Highpointe College geology department, and Anita Archer here for tea this afternoon," Maggie said aloud.

My mistress didn't talk to herself. I moved closer. This was peculiar.

"I wonder which tea service I should use." She opened the upper cabinet that held our collection of tea service items. She picked up an ornate silver coffeepot and turned it over in her hands.

I recoiled in horror. Surely she knew that was a coffee pot, not a teapot. I hovered over her shoulder and focused my attention on our Royal Winton tea service in the Summertime pattern. Its bold, all-over chintz design—filled with roses, daisies, violets, and forget-me-nots in bright pinks, blues, yellows, and greens on a creamy background—is what I would've chosen for an informal yet intimate gathering of three ladies.

"I think this colorful set would be best for a dreary day like today," she said. She lifted a plate from the stack and turned it over. "Royal Winton—Summertime," she read the backstamp. "I think it's so cheerful, don't you, Alistair?"

I jumped back as if I'd seen a ghost.

"I can sense you, you know," she said. "I've never used this tea set in all my years at Rosemont. When I entered the pantry, I intended to choose the Portmeirion Botanic Garden. I picked up that silver coffee pot to see if it needed polishing, and suddenly I had an overwhelming urge to select the Royal Winton."

She spun around, and we were suddenly nose-to-nose.

"I trust your judgment, Alistair. I think the chintz tea service will be just the thing. John gave me a tin of Lady Londonderry tea for Christmas. I plan to serve it, along with a plate of freshly baked currant scones." She turned back to the cupboard and began removing the teapot, sugar bowl, creamer, and three plates, teacups, and saucers.

"There's a cucumber and a brick of cream cheese in the refrigerator. I hard-boiled eggs this morning, and I have a baked chicken breast left over from last night's dinner. I'll make cucumber, chicken salad, and egg salad tea sandwiches."

Maggie stacked up the dishes and began ferrying them to the kitchen.

"I know you won't approve," she said, "but I'm going to thaw a package of frozen mini cream puffs that I keep on hand in the freezer."

She was correct. I did not approve.

"They're really yummy, and they're the only thing I've got on hand as something sweet for the final course. I wish we hadn't eaten all of the sugar cookies I brought home." She returned to the butler's pantry. "Now," she said, "do I have a tiered tea stand in here to serve all this on? Alistair, surely you must know."

Well, of course we had tiered stands. We had several of them. If she took six steps diagonally to her right and opened the bottom cupboard, she would find them lined up along the back.

Maggie stood in the middle of the room as if waiting for my guidance.

I was not about to let her down.

The top hinge on the appropriate cupboard door gave way, and the door sagged, held in place only by the bottom hinge.

Maggie crossed to the cupboard and found the tiered stand that matched the china she had selected. She spun around to face the room, clutching her chest.

"I knew it! John thinks I'm imagining things, but this proves it." Her smile matched the gladness in my heart. She knew I was here—and *I* knew *she* knew.

"I think you've been protecting me since the first night I came to Rosemont during that blizzard. *You* brought me Eve the next morning. *You* helped me get out of the attic when I was locked in it. *You* directed us to that Thomas Cole painting and the valuable silver we sold to raise the money we needed to buy out Frank Hayes' share of Rosemont. I'm sure there are many other things you did for us. I want you to know that I'm grateful," Maggie said. She turned in a circle and looked into every corner of the room. "Thank you, Alistair."

We both remained motionless, savoring the moment.

"And now I'd better get busy in the kitchen. I'm serving tea this afternoon."

I followed close behind her. This ordinary day had become extraordinary.

CHAPTER 9

Fiona took a sip of her tea and rested the cup on its saucer. She nestled into the overstuffed chair, drawn close to the fire. "This has been the most pleasant afternoon I've spent in years," she said. "I can't tell you how much I've enjoyed myself, Maggie. Thank you for going to all this effort." She gestured toward the tea trolley covered with an embroidered cloth. The tiered china stand now stood empty, except for two cream puffs.

"It was my pleasure," Maggie said. "I had so much fun doing this. Sitting with you this afternoon in my library lets me imagine what life must've been like at Rosemont over a hundred years ago. Instead of afternoon tea being a special occasion, it would have been a daily occurrence."

"It's a shame our modern lives are so busy that we've gotten away from this ritual," Anita said. "I arrived here two hours ago feeling agitated and unsettled." She gave Fiona a rueful smile. "I have to admit, your proposal upset me. I had the wrong impression of what's about to happen."

"I understand why you did," Fiona said. "I'm so sorry—almost a page and a half of explanation got dropped from the proposal I sent you." She scooted to the edge of her chair and leaned toward Anita. "I hope you feel better about things now."

"I do," Anita replied. "I'm relieved that there will only be a handful of people on site at any given time. It never occurred to me that so many people would volunteer for the excavation."

"Every senior in the geology department wants to participate," Fiona said. "The opportunity to excavate a prehistoric creature is extremely rare. I didn't have the heart to turn anyone down. The fairest way to proceed is to give everyone a chance. I'll be on site whenever our crew is there, and my colleague from the Joseph Moore Museum will also be present occasionally. The rest of the volunteers will work in four-hour shifts. We'll operate two shifts a day."

"That makes perfect sense," Anita said.

"If the only thing we excavate is that mastodon tusk, we'll finish in a matter of days," Fiona said. "We'll search for additional skeletal remains. If we don't find any, we'll be out of your hair by the end of the week. If we uncover more, we'll keep going—and I'll let you know immediately."

"That sounds good to me," Anita said. "I hope you come across more. It would be so exciting for the college."

Fiona cleared her throat and glanced between Maggie

and Anita. "About that. Have either of you talked to Alex Scanlon lately?"

"The mayor hasn't said a word to me," Anita said. "Maggie, you and Alex are close friends. Have you heard from him?"

Maggie shook her head. "What does Alex have to do with this?"

Fiona placed her hands on her knees. "Mayor Scanlon believes Westbury should own the remains."

Maggie and Anita snapped their heads toward each other, then back at Fiona. "Why?" Maggie asked.

"Let me clarify," Fiona said. "If all we find is the tusk, Alex is on board with it being displayed at the college. But if we find more remains—if we can piece together an entire skeleton—he'd like it to be displayed in a natural history museum on the square."

"We don't have a natural history museum on the square—or anywhere else in Westbury," Anita pointed out.

"I know," Fiona said, "but he thinks the town should acquire the other vacant buildings on the square and turn them into museum spaces. He mentioned a quilting museum—or ones dedicated to buttons and threads. Those would fit nicely with Stitches in Time. He suggested a museum for ships in a bottle, one for toothpick sculptures, and a museum devoted to coins and stamps. There could even be an insect museum. Anything related to a popular hobby would be a good candidate." She looked at Anita. "Alex told me that your sewing machine museum inspired him."

"I heard he's been investigating ways to revitalize the

town square," Maggie said. "I didn't realize that making it into a museum district was under consideration."

"He said he just came up with the idea," Fiona replied. "He hasn't discussed it with the town council yet. Alex contacted me to 'put a bug in my ear,' as he put it. If we find an entire mastodon skeleton, he said that would be the time to introduce the idea to the council." She looked at Maggie. "What do you think?"

"As a former mayor of Westbury, I think the idea has a lot of merit. Museum districts are popular attractions. Bringing more people to the square will benefit the existing restaurants and shops—and draw new ones."

"I was a museum studies major in college," Anita said. "I never finished my degree because I came home to help run Celebrations when my mother became ill. That's why I'm so thrilled about opening the sewing machine museum. People think of big museums like the Smithsonian or the Louvre—but those are extremely expensive to operate and maintain. Gordon opened my eyes to the financial viability of a small museum with a unique focus."

"Do you expect to make a profit at Stitches in Time?" Maggie asked.

"Gordon and I have a business plan that shows me in the black in my second year," Anita said.

"That's terrific," Fiona replied. "I thought we'd open a natural history museum at Highpointe if we found an entire skeleton. But I realize I don't have the budget for that and would have to raise significant funds to make it happen."

"I was thinking the same thing," Maggie said. "The woman replacing Josh as my assistant when he graduates has experience with fundraising. I figured we'd tap into her expertise."

"Would that mean we'd compete with Frank Haynes's efforts to raise money for Forever Guides?"

"Good point," Maggie said. "Forever Guides has generous benefactors, but I think Frank will need to raise funds from the community, too. I'd hate to step on his toes."

"Alex talked about that," Fiona said. "He said a municipality has tax revenues and other funding options that make it more feasible for Westbury to make a home for a mastodon if we find one."

"Again," Maggie said, "he's right about that." She leaned forward in her chair. "This is fascinating. My mind is racing."

Fiona took another sip of her tea. "Basically, his suggestions focused on museums devoted to popular hobbies or things from the past that people are still interested in today. His vision extends to museums that offer classes for children and adults. He sees Museum Row as a vibrant place where people come, not just to look at things, but to have hands-on experiences learning new skills."

"I'm loving this more and more," Maggie said.

"I plan to offer classes in sewing machine repair and restoration at Stitches in Time," Anita said. "I don't know how popular they'll be, but I get calls every month at my bridal shop from people who know I collect and restore vintage sewing machines, asking for advice."

Maggie closed her eyes and held her hands up, palms out. "I can picture it. The whole side of the square near Stitches in Time will bustle on the weekends. Parents will be pushing strollers on the sidewalks, dogs will be racing around the square, and the restaurants and shops ringing the museum district will be packed."

"Their arms full of purchases from the gift shops," Anita added.

Fiona chuckled. "I see it, too."

"I wonder why Alex didn't mention it to me," Maggie said. "I ran into him at Pete's last week, and he never said a word."

"I think he didn't want to get too far down the road until he knew if we actually had an entire skeleton." Fiona bit her lower lip. "He also wanted to discuss something else."

Maggie raised an eyebrow.

"Alex asked if I would run the natural history museum if Westbury moves forward with one."

Maggie rested her hands on her knees and looked at Fiona. "What did you tell him?"

"That I love being head of the geology department at Highpointe," Fiona said. "It's my dream job, and I won't leave it. But, I have to admit, being in charge of a museum I get to build from the ground up is a close second."

"Maybe you could do both," Maggie said. "I'd hate to lose you as dean, but, if we removed some of your teaching responsibilities, you could stay on part-time with us in that capacity and work part-time at the new museum." She leaned back in her chair. "We're getting ahead of ourselves. We don't need to figure that out now."

"I agree," Fiona said. "I feel so much better having told you both about this. In fact, that's why I made the mistake on the proposal. My mind was spinning after Alex and I finished talking. I mistakenly sent you a prior draft and not the final version. Again—I'm so sorry."

"I'm not," Anita said. "If you hadn't, the three of us wouldn't have gotten together for tea this afternoon."

"I agree," Maggie said. "I loved spending time with both of you, and I'm excited about the possibility of a museum district on the square."

"Now all we have to do is find a mastodon skeleton," Fiona chuckled.

"Fingers crossed," Anita said.

"My crew and I will be there Wednesday morning at eight," Fiona said.

"I'll be ready and waiting," Anita replied.

"I love it when a plan comes together," Maggie said. "But one thing remains."

Fiona and Anita looked at her.

"There are two tiny cream puffs left—one for each of you."

"I'm stuffed," Anita said.

"Me too," Fiona replied. She looked at the fireplace, where Eve and Roman slept in their baskets by the hearth. "I know your husband is a vet, and dogs aren't supposed to get people food … but can we?"

"As long as you promise not to tell John," Maggie replied, "I think they deserve a treat, too."

Roman and Eve stirred and got to their feet, sensing—as dogs often do—when someone is talking about them.

Fiona and Anita each grabbed a cream puff and tossed it toward the hearth—and the open mouths of the eager dogs.

CHAPTER 10

Rain pelted the car windows as Josh and Sunday pulled to the curb in front of Judy's former home. Josh cut the engine, and the hammering of the precipitation that had continued nonstop for the past three days replaced the thwack of the windshield wipers.

"At least we'll know pretty quickly if the roof is solid," Josh said.

Sunday responded with a thin-lipped smile.

"Are you nervous about seeing the house?" Josh asked.

She nodded. "I know it's ridiculous—if we don't like it, we'll keep looking—but, frankly, I've been lusting after this property for years. If it disappoints, I'll be heartbroken."

He reached for her hand and squeezed it. "I know you've got your hopes up, sweetheart. But I also know you're far tougher than you give yourself credit for. If this isn't the one, you'll put it out of your mind, and we'll continue searching. We'll find our forever home."

Sunday nodded and released her seatbelt. She pulled the hood of her raincoat over her head.

"Ready?" he asked.

She gripped the strap of the purse hanging from her shoulder and got out of the car.

The arched mahogany front door with the speakeasy window opened, and Tim hurried down the steps and along the winding walkway leading from the sidewalk to the house. He held a large red umbrella over his head and extended it toward Sunday.

She ducked under its cover, and the three of them made their way to the meager protection of the portico. Tim pushed the door open and stepped aside for Sunday and Josh to precede him into the house.

They stood on an industrial-looking carpet runner in the foyer and allowed rain to drip from their jackets.

"I carry one of these to protect the floors if I'm showing a house while it's raining," Tim said, pointing to the runner. "These are original hardwood floors. The narrow slats tell you they're from the 1920s, when the house was built."

Sunday bent and looked at the floor. "These slats are beautiful—and in great shape. I'm glad you're protecting them. Is there somewhere to leave our jackets while we look around? I don't want to drip water everywhere."

Tim pointed to a large plastic tote along the wall. "Fold them and store them there."

They removed their jackets and placed them in the tote.

"I'm going to take my shoes off, too," Sunday said. "They're soaked."

Josh and Tim did the same.

"I'll tell you about the house, and then the two of you can explore on your own," Tim said. "It's 2,700 square feet with three bedrooms and two and a half baths. There's a living room, dining room, eat-in kitchen, a small library that Judy used as her office, and a large sunroom. The washer and dryer are in a laundry room in the basement. The water heater and furnace are down there too, along with a large, unfinished room. The basement has four-foot-tall windows on every side, so there's plenty of natural light. You could turn that unfinished space into one—or several—pleasant rooms."

Josh glanced at Sunday. "Like a workout room, home theater, or playroom," he said, smiling at her.

"There are a few pieces of furniture Judy didn't move to the Olsson House, and she's willing to leave them for you, if you want them. If not, she'll sell them," Tim continued. "I'll wait for you here. Take your time. Judy's available by phone if you have questions."

"I have one before we start," Josh said. "Do you know how old the roof is? And what about updates to the kitchen or bathrooms? Did Judy redo the plumbing and wiring?"

"Great questions," Tim said. "Judy told me she put on a new roof four years ago and updated the kitchen with new appliances and countertops five years ago. She refinished the original cabinets because they're solid wood and better than those she could buy today. She's maintained everything in top working order, but the bathrooms were last redone in the '80s, so you might want to update those."

"Good to know," Josh said. "I don't mind outdated décor, but . . ." He glanced at his wife.

"Having a few projects might be fun," Sunday said. "I watch those DIY shows, and it doesn't look all that hard—as long as everything's in good working order so we don't have to tackle anything right away."

"Then you've got nothing to worry about," Tim said.

"All right," Josh said, taking Sunday's hand. "Let the tour begin."

A large rectangular opening on their left led into the living room. Rough-hewn beams ran the width of the room. The diamond-paned window visible from the sidewalk was set deep into the wall, flanked by built-in bookcases. A thick cushion was fitted into the deep windowsill.

Sunday brought her hand to her heart. "A window seat! I've always wanted a window seat." She crossed the room for a closer look. "We can see the Olsson House from here. What a beautiful view!" She fingered the drapes hanging on either side. "I love the tone-on-tone of this creamy windowpane check. And the deep taupe on the bookshelves is stunning against the lighter walls. They look beautiful with these dark wood floors."

"The fireplace on the outside wall is impressive," Josh said.

"Isn't it?" Sunday replied. "That mantel is a showstopper. The symmetrical carvings on the side panels are lovely. It's painted the same creamy enamel they used on the crown molding, baseboards, and window trim. This little one-story house may be smaller than the others on the street, but it has the high-end details of its grander neighbors."

They retraced their steps to the center hallway and proceeded to the dining room behind the living room.

Two generous diamond-paned windows sat on the outside wall, surrounding a built-in china hutch. An antique Chippendale table and eight chairs occupied the center.

"They've brought the same color scheme into this room," Sunday said. "It's absolutely perfect."

Josh nodded in agreement.

They opened a pocket door at the far end of the room, revealing the kitchen.

Solid wood cabinets in a medium brown tone lined three sides. A farmhouse sink sat beneath a large casement window overlooking the yard. A six-burner gas range with double ovens stood opposite the sink. White marble countertops and classic subway tile complemented the cabinetry. Identical beams to those in the living and dining rooms ran the length of the ceiling.

Sunday stepped into the room. "This isn't the biggest kitchen I've ever seen—but it's the most charming." She pointed to the lower cabinets next to the dishwasher. "I love these open cubbies for baskets. I'll store potatoes and onions in them. And the cabinets reach all the way to the ceiling, so there's a ton of storage."

Josh stretched his arm over his head as he looked up. "I'd say these are nine-foot ceilings. If you put anything in those upper cabinets, you'll need a stepladder to get at them."

"That's fine," she said. "We'll store stuff there that we don't use very often—Christmas dishes, turkey platters, parfait glasses, vases."

"Do we have any of that stuff?" he asked.

She playfully cuffed his shoulder. "Maybe not—but we will. And there's plenty of room to store everything here." She opened a cupboard. "Look—the shelves are adjustable!"

"Good to know." Josh opened and shut another cabinet. "These close nice and snug. They're quality cabinets."

Sunday's smile widened. She walked to the sink, opened the dishwasher on her left, then pantomimed taking dishes from the right-hand side of the sink, rinsing them, and placing them into the dishwasher. "Perfect flow," she said over her shoulder.

A round breakfast table and four chairs sat by a large window in an alcove off the kitchen.

"Judy's also leaving the breakfast table," Josh remarked.

"I love it!" Sunday exclaimed. "It's the perfect size. The view of the yard from this big window is lovely, too."

"I think we should take bets on how many times you'll say the word 'lovely,'" Josh teased.

"That would be silly," Sunday said. "I could change it up and say beautiful, charming, perfect, or my dream come true."

Josh took her in his arms. "You're smitten, aren't you?"

"Hopelessly in love, I'm afraid. You?"

"We haven't seen the bedrooms or bathrooms yet, so I'm reserving judgment."

They returned to the hallway. A door on the left led to a

simple powder room. The last room on that side of the house was a sunroom.

"This must've been a screened-in porch back in the day," Sunday said, pointing to the large double-hung windows that lined the room on two sides. "Someone added these recently."

"This is pleasant," Josh commented. "Light and cheery—even on a dreary day like today."

They crossed the hall and entered a bedroom with a large window overlooking the side yard. A closet stood opposite the window. A door led into a Jack-and-Jill bathroom, which connected to an identical bedroom.

"These would be great kids' rooms. You could even fit bunk beds in them," Josh said. "Way nicer than what I had growing up."

"Me too," Sunday said. "They'd be just fine."

The next room was half the size, with one small window and no closet. The walls were lined with empty bookshelves.

"This must be the library," Sunday said. "We could use it as a home office. It'd be perfect for that."

"I agree," Josh replied. "Now for the master bedroom."

They walked into the room at the front of the house, on the right side of the entry. Like the living room, it featured exposed ceiling beams. A smaller version of the living room fireplace stood on the outside wall.

Sunday placed her palms on either side of her head. "I must be dreaming. A fireplace in my bedroom?" She turned to Josh wide-eyed. "I'm ready to sign on the dotted line."

Josh walked to two doors on the wall at the other end of

the room. One led to a small walk-in closet and the other to a compact but nicely appointed bathroom.

"These might pose a problem," he said. "I've seen your closet—you already have more clothes than would fit in here."

She stepped in and out of both spaces. "You're right. They're not ideal." She faced him, eyes shining. "But they're the only negatives we've seen. We can live with this for now and get creative later."

"I guess we could expand into the library, later on," he replied

"Exactly," she said, snapping her fingers. "That would solve the issue."

"If we need home offices, we can put them in the basement," Josh added.

"Genius idea!" Sunday clasped her hands. "I hope this works out. I'll be crushed if it doesn't."

"We haven't seen the entire house yet," Josh reminded her. "Let's check out the basement and backyard. We're not buying a house without looking at every square inch."

"You're right," Sunday said, taking his hand. "There's a door in the breakfast room we didn't open—I bet it leads to the basement."

They completed their tour of the basement and returned to Tim, who waited patiently by the front door. He watched them approach and smiled—he'd been in the real estate business long enough to know when someone had fallen in love with a house.

He reached for their coats. "Ready to see the backyard and garage?"

Sunday stepped into her shoes and slipped on her jacket.

"I think we'd better," Josh said.

Tim put on his coat and grabbed his umbrella. "Let's go out the back," he said, leading the way.

Josh took Sunday's hand, and they followed him.

"It already feels like home," Sunday whispered.

CHAPTER 11

Anita walked from her office at the back of Archer's Bridal to the front window and stared across the square at the future home of Stitches in Time. She had unlocked the building for Fiona and her crew of volunteers at eight that morning, then driven through the pouring rain to her customary parking spot behind the bridal shop. She'd kept an eye on the museum entrance, but there had been nothing to see.

The workroom supervisor walked up behind her and placed an arm around Anita's shoulders. "You've gone from your office to the window so many times this morning you're going to wear a path in the floor," she teased. "I thought you said they would bring things in and out through the back door."

Anita nodded. "That's right. I don't know why I keep looking over there. I know I won't see anything."

"You're curious about what's going on," Louise said. "Frankly, so are the rest of us." She gestured to the seamstresses at work behind them. "It's your building—why don't you go over there and find out? The rain's let up." She pointed out the window to a sliver of blue sky peeking through the clouds. "The forecast predicts more heavy rain this afternoon, but it looks like you could dash over now without getting drenched."

"You think I should?" Anita turned to her.

"Absolutely. We're in good shape here. Go on."

Anita nodded and stepped out the door onto the wet pavement. After days of nonstop rain, the storefronts and sidewalks around the square gleamed, as if freshly power-washed. She crossed the street and walked on the path that bisected the square. Fat drops of water dripped onto her head from the canopy of trees. The square stood deserted on this midweek morning.

Anita opened the door to Stitches in Time. The first floor was empty, but excited voices echoed from the basement. The door to it stood open, and construction lights being used in the excavation illuminated the opening.

She walked to the basement door and intercepted Sam as he came down the steps from the second floor.

"I wondered if I'd see you here today," Sam said. "I know how busy you are at the bridal shop, but I hoped you'd have time to break away."

"To tell you the truth," Anita said, "all I've been thinking about the entire morning is the excavation. I've been pacing from my office to the front window on a continuous loop. I finally decided to come over and check on things." She tilted her head and looked at him. "What are you doing here today? I thought the renovation couldn't proceed until you received the tile that's on back order."

"I told Jeff I was coming over to make sure our new roof wasn't leaking," Sam said with a sheepish shrug. "Which I know is ridiculous because I checked it the last two days, and it's been fine, so I know there aren't any problems. And you and I both know I really came to see how the dig was going."

"I'm excited to see the progress, too. Have you been down there yet?"

"I went upstairs first to make sure the roof didn't leak, since that was the excuse I used," he replied. "I was about to head downstairs."

"Let's do it then," she said enthusiastically.

They walked to the basement door together.

"After you," Sam said.

Anita descended halfway down the steps with Sam at her heels. The air was dank and cool. The energy of the excavation crew in the basement was electric. The dig site—a ten-foot square area—was cordoned off by yellow caution tape. It was brightly lit, while the rest of the basement receded into shadow.

Fiona leaned over, demonstrating to two of her student volunteers how to carefully hammer wooden stakes into the ground at measured intervals. She instructed them to tie twine between the stakes to create a tight, evenly spaced grid.

"We'll catalog and map each square to ensure we document the location of every bone or artifact we find," Fiona explained. She turned and caught sight of Anita and Sam on the stairs.

"Good morning!" Anita called. "How's it going?"

"We're getting everything set up," Fiona replied. "This is a formal dig, as we discussed on Monday. That means we'll proceed slowly and methodically to examine every bit of this soil."

"Of course," Anita said. "How much more do you have to do before you start working on the tusk?"

Fiona pointed to a low table near the bottom of the stairs, positioned outside the taped-off area, where two other students were busy unpacking items from a plastic tote. "We're setting up our field notebooks, digital calipers, labeled specimen bags, and a tablet running 3D imaging software on that table."

She moved to a second tote and lifted the lid. "Here we've got a small sprayer and a bucket for mixing our consolidant —that's a paleontologist's version of glue. We're waiting for a delivery to my office of one of the necessary ingredients. There's also foil, plaster, and burlap. The only thing left to bring in from the truck is a boom-mounted scanner we'll rig to hover over the grid and map the excavation in high resolution."

Anita and Sam both leaned over the railing to get a better look.

"This is quite an operation," Sam commented.

"Indeed, it is," Fiona replied. "I didn't sleep a wink last night—I'm so eager to get started."

One student nodded. “I didn’t sleep either.”

“Do you mind if we watch?” Anita asked.

“This is painstaking work,” Fiona replied. “We’ll go through the soil inch by inch with the proverbial fine-tooth comb. I’m afraid it will bore you stiff.”

Anita and Sam’s crestfallen expressions looked like they’d just missed the last bus of the day.

Fiona softened. “We’ll know when we’re getting close to something,” she said. “I’ll text you both when we do. You can come over to watch from the stairs if you’d like.”

Their faces brightened, as if they'd caught that last bus.

“Keep a close eye on your phones this afternoon,” Fiona said. “We’ll start with the tusk. With luck, we’ll have most of it exposed by the end of the day.”

CHAPTER 12

Josh carried two medium-sized moving boxes into Sunday's living room and stacked them with his other boxes along one wall. "That's everything," he said.

"You weren't kidding when you said you travel light," Sunday replied. "If I were moving into your place, I'd have four times as much stuff."

Josh made a show of looking around the room, his gaze landing on her decorative pillows, pictures, vases, knickknacks, books, and cozy throws. "That's because I don't have any of this stuff," he said. "Just the basics."

"Well, you've got it now," Sunday said, grinning. "It's these touches that make a house a home."

"I agree," Josh said. "You've got a good eye for decor."

"Is there anything packed in these boxes you need to use right away?"

Josh shook his head. "I brought my clothes, my laptop, and school books over earlier. That's all I really need for now."

"You planned to unpack everything while you're off on spring break, but would you mind waiting until we hear if Judy accepted our offer?"

"Good thinking," he said. "If she does, I'd have to repack everything. I'll wait—if you don't mind having boxes stacked in your living room." He headed into the kitchen for a glass of water. Every cupboard door stood open, and a jumble of mismatched coffee mugs covered the kitchen table. He pulled a glass from a cabinet, filled it at the tap, and carried it into the living room. "What's going on in there?" he asked, motioning to the kitchen, as Sunday straightened his stack of boxes.

"I'm purging," she said. "I should've done it earlier so there'd be room for your kitchen items, but, now that we might be moving, it seemed like a good time to go through everything."

Josh helped her realign the last of the boxes, then pulled her into his arms.

"You're full steam ahead on this, aren't you?"

"Sure am," she said. "I can't help myself. Sitting around here waiting for news from Tim is torture. I decided to do something productive. Whether we end up with Judy's house or not, my kitchen drawers and cupboards need decluttering."

"I noticed on my way over here that the rain finally stopped," Josh said. "It's still overcast—and looks like it might start again soon—but a few rays of sunshine have managed to peek through. I thought this would be a great time to let the dogs stretch their legs. Dan and Cara have been cooped up inside for days with only the briefest bathroom breaks. I'll take them for a long walk before it rains again. Want to come with?"

"That's a wonderful idea," Sunday said. "But do you mind if I pass? I'm on a roll with this kitchen project, and I'd like to finish before it's time to start dinner."

"Perfectly fine," Josh said. "What are you going to do with the stuff you don't want to keep?"

"I plan to donate it to the hospital thrift shop."

"Set it aside, and I'll drop it off after our walk." He headed to the coat rack by the front door and lifted the dogs' harnesses from their hooks.

The dogs, who had been sleeping on their beds in the corner, sprang to their feet and trotted over to him.

"Do you want to get out of here?" he asked, fitting Dan into his harness. "Have you got cabin fever, Cara?" he added, securing her gear.

Sunday walked them to the door. She gave Josh a kiss and bent to rub each dog's ears. "Have fun, you guys," she said.

"You too, sweetheart," Josh said. "I have a feeling you're enjoying this. Please don't knock yourself out. If you can't finish before dinner, we'll order a pizza."

"We did that last night," Sunday said, giving him a sidelong glance.

"I can eat pizza every night," he said. "In fact, as a bachelor, I often did."

"I'm glad you're not picky," Sunday said. "But once a week is my limit."

Dan whimpered and pawed at the door.

"My offer still stands," Josh said. "We'll go out for something else." Then he opened the door, and the three of them stepped out into the thin sunshine.

Sunday returned to the kitchen and attacked her project with gusto. She was on the third rung of a stepladder when her phone began to ring in the other room. She put the turkey roaster back in the cabinet, and quickly descended the stepstool.

She dashed into the living room and lunged for her phone. The screen displayed Tim Knudsen's name. Sunday swiped to answer. "Hey, Tim," she said, huffing.

"You sound out of breath," he replied. "Am I calling at a bad time?"

"No," she quickly assured him. "I was up on a stepstool, cleaning out the tall cupboards in my kitchen. I had to climb down and run for the phone."

"Sounds like a productive use of your time," Tim said. "You're about to be doing a lot more of that."

Sunday sucked in her breath and held it.

"I'm calling to let you know Judy has accepted your offer."

Sunday gasped. "With no conditions or counteroffers?"

"None," Tim said. "She feels you were very fair."

"I'm glad you know the square-foot sales price for the area," Sunday said. "We want to be fair to her."

"And she wants to be fair to you, too," Tim replied.

"You told us that other buyers would probably be willing to pay more than we offered just to get the lot," Sunday said.

"Judy's had multiple offers over the years from buyers who planned to demolish the house and build something new. They were after the lot, not the home. She never sold to any of them because she said it would break her heart to see the house torn down. She was delighted to accept your offer because she knows you'll live in the house and love it as much as she does."

Sunday's voice cracked with emotion. "I almost can't believe this."

"When would you and Josh like to come in to get the paperwork started?" he asked. "Judy will accept your down payment, and she'll carry back a thirty-year loan on the balance. If you ever decide to refinance, you can."

Sunday sank onto the sofa, not trusting her wobbly knees. "That's phenomenal," she said.

"There is one more thing Judy wanted me to tell you," Tim added. "Closing of escrow will be in thirty days, as you stipulated in your offer—but she's willing to grant you pre-possession rights so you can move your things in ahead of time."

"Oh my gosh," Sunday cried. "That would be so helpful. I can't wait to see her and thank her in person."

"I'm sure she'd love that," Tim said. "She's thrilled that you and Josh are going to own her home and be across-the-street neighbors. When can we get together to sign papers?"

"Josh is out walking the dogs," Sunday said. "But I'm certain we'd both like to get this going as soon as possible."

"How about my office at nine tomorrow morning?" Tim asked.

"We'll be there," Sunday replied. "And Tim—thank you so much for your part in making our dream come true."

She ended the call and ran into the bedroom. Sunday shoved her feet into the first pair of sneakers she could find and rushed out the front door. She knew the path Josh took when he walked the dogs. This news couldn't wait until he got home. She jogged to the end of the block and turned right. Two blocks ahead, she spotted the familiar figure of her husband and their two dogs. Sunday waved her arms in a wide arc over her head and broke into a run.

Josh waved back. The dogs saw her and strained at their leashes to get to her.

"We got it!" she yelled when they were only half a block apart.

Josh quickened his stride, and Sunday flung herself into his arms.

"We've got our forever home," she cried, pressing her face into his neck.

He pulled her into a tight embrace, and they clung to each other. Cara and Dan, sensing something momentous was happening, pranced at their feet. When they finally pulled apart, Sunday took a deep breath and filled him in on the details as they walked back to her place.

"I can't wait to see Tim tomorrow and make it official," Josh said. "In the meantime, I'm ready to start packing."

"Under the circumstances," Sunday said, grinning up at

him, "I think ordering a pizza for dinner again is a wonderful idea."

CHAPTER 13

Anita handed the credit card back to the mother of the bride. "Thank you for choosing Archer's Bridal," she said. "We stand behind our work, so, if you have any problems, please call."

"I can't believe the wedding is a week from Saturday," the woman said. "We've been planning it for more than a year—which seemed like plenty of time—but we still have so much to do."

Anita lifted the voluminous gown, secured in its garment bag, from the hook by the register. "Where are you parked?" she asked. "I'll carry this to your car for you."

"I'm out front—two doors down."

Anita followed her to the car and helped her lay the gown across the back seat.

"Have a beautiful day," Anita said. "The next time you're in the area, I'd love to see photos."

"I'll stop in," the woman replied and got into her car.

Anita checked her watch. It was a few minutes past four. She had kept her phone in her pocket the entire afternoon, waiting for the text from Fiona that never came. She pulled it out to check again—still nothing.

The break in the rain had continued, but the skies were dark again. It looked as if the clouds were about to burst. She should go back into the shop for her jacket—or at least grab an umbrella. Instead, she crossed the square at a rapid pace. The excavation hours were officially 8 to 4, and she hoped she hadn't missed Fiona before she left. If that meant walking in the rain, so be it.

The first fat drops fell on her head as she made her way across the square. A banner in the front window of her building bore the silhouette of a vintage sewing machine, with the words *Stitches in Time: Linking the Past to the Present* in a circle around the outline. The words *Coming Soon* in red ink were displayed below the image. She lunged for the front door as the rain fell harder. It was locked. Her heart sank. Fiona must have gone home without giving her an update.

Anita scolded herself for not bringing her keys. She was impulsive and impatient—and look where that got her. She'd be soaked by the time she got back to the bridal shop. Anita turned, bent her head against the steady wall of rain, and took a step toward the curb.

The door to Stitches in Time opened.

"Anita!" Fiona called, raising her voice above the rising wind.

Anita spun around and hurried to the door.

"One of my students told me he saw you heading over," Fiona said.

Anita stepped inside, and Fiona pushed the door shut against the storm.

"I was just about to text you and Sam," she said.

Rain dripped from Anita's hair and ran inside her collar. "I guess I should've waited for that," she said. "I looked at the time and was afraid I'd miss you, so I dashed over as the rain started again."

"I should've gotten in touch with you both earlier," Fiona admitted. "It was too optimistic to think we'd finish uncovering the tusk early this afternoon."

"Is everything okay?"

"Yes. It's taking a bit longer to excavate than I thought," Fiona said. "The portion that remains buried is more fragile than I expected based on what is exposed." She caught Anita's concerned look and clarified. "That just means we've had to move more slowly. I'm confident we'll have the tusk fully uncovered by mid-morning tomorrow, and I'll text you and Sam then."

"Great," Anita said.

"I'm sorry I got your hopes up."

"When will you pull the whole thing out of the ground?" Anita asked.

"Given its delicate condition, I think it'll take us two or three days to strengthen it with consolidant. It shows quite a few cracks and gaps. Once we take care of those, we'll use burlap to make a plaster cast to stabilize the tusk before we move it. You'll be able to see it tomorrow, but, once it's cast, there's not much to look at. We'll move it to the college to dry under controlled conditions and apply additional consolidant there. That process will take weeks—or months."

"So the best time to see anything will be tomorrow," Anita reiterated. "And the removal will probably be the middle of next week?"

Fiona nodded. "I'll be sure to let you and Sam know exactly when."

"I'd like to see it come out of the ground, too," Anita said. "To be honest, I'm fascinated by the entire process."

"Then I'll make sure you know everything as soon as I do," Fiona promised. "Should I send you a progress report at the end of each day? I don't want you running over here in the pouring rain again."

"I'd appreciate that," Anita said, tucking her wet hair behind her ears. "Are you the only one here?"

"Everyone else has left for the day. My student called me when I was headed out the back. I figured you were coming to the front door, so I came to let you in."

"Thank you," Anita said. "I'll let you get going. See you tomorrow." She turned toward the door.

"I'll give you a ride to the bridal shop," Fiona said, heading to the rear door. "I'm not about to turn you out in this."

Anita followed her. A crack of lightning split the sky overhead, followed directly by the deep boom of thunder.

Fiona unlocked her Jeep with the key fob, and both women dashed through the rain to the car.

ANITA PULLED her bowl of reheated chicken noodle soup from the microwave and carried it to the kitchen island. It was the last of the batch she'd made on Monday. She loved her grandmother's homemade recipe, but, after eating the same thing every night that week, she was glad to be done with it. She had planned to make herself a salad to go with it but didn't feel like making the effort. Instead, she pulled a sleeve of saltines from the pantry, grabbed a spoon from the drawer, and plunked herself down on the stool in front of the soup.

She placed her cell phone on the counter beside her—while she stirred the soup to cool it—and opened her messages. Gordon still hadn't responded to the text she'd sent that morning, the one where she told him she expected to see the tusk this afternoon.

She knew he was working long hours with his best client, but it wasn't like him not to reply. He'd at least send a quick reaction to her texts—especially one about the excavation, which he'd been so interested in from the beginning.

Anita crumbled a handful of crackers into her soup and ate her dinner without enthusiasm. She told herself she had no reason to be down in the dumps. Fiona and her crew were being extremely careful. She'd see the tusk tomorrow. The delay was no big deal. And Gordon must've had a very busy day. They'd talk at bedtime, like they always did.

She finished her dinner, loaded her bowl and spoon into the dishwasher, and settled into her favorite chair with the book she was reading for book club. The novel was a light, breezy rom-com, and she was enjoying it. She'd read until Gordon called.

But Gordon never called.

Anita woke an hour after their usual time to talk. She closed her book that lay open on her chest and set it on the end table. She considered calling Gordon but decided against it. If he were working that hard, she didn't want to disturb him. She and Gordon had talked every day for months. Surely, she'd get a text—or a call—from him in the morning. There was no reason to worry.

ANITA SAT AT HER DESK, engulfed in stacks of invoices and receipts. She'd been trying to reconcile the bridal shop's bank statement for the past hour—a routine task that should've taken thirty minutes. But she couldn't concentrate and had to go back over entries a second time.

Even though she'd gone to bed later than usual, she'd woken up early. Before even getting out of bed, she grabbed her phone from the nightstand and checked for a message from Gordon. Nothing. No missed calls either.

She scrolled to his number and hesitated. She felt annoyed and out of sorts. If he was working around the clock, which was the most logical explanation, she didn't want to be whiny or demanding. She decided to call him later in the day, after the mastodon tusk had been exposed.

Satisfied with that plan, Anita had gotten up and started

her day. She went to work and was on her third pass through the bank statement when her phone chirped with an incoming text.

It's time!!! Fiona's simple message was directed to her and Sam.

Anita stacked the receipts in a pile on her desk and secured them with a stapler. The bank statement would have to wait.

She headed for the door, telling Louise she was going to see the exposed tusk.

The woman narrowed her eyes. "I thought this was the big reveal you've been waiting for."

"It is," Anita replied.

"After weeks of eager anticipation, you appear as excited as if you were going in for a root canal."

Anita took a deep breath. "I'm just tired, that's all. I didn't sleep well last night."

"Ahh," the woman said. "Please take pictures. All of us want to see it."

Anita nodded and made the short walk to Stitches in Time. Sam was waiting for her at the top of the stairs to the basement.

"I wanted you to have the first look," he said.

"That's thoughtful of you, Sam," Anita said. They descended together.

Fiona knelt on the ground behind a tusk that curved upward in a graceful arch. The base was larger in diameter than her thigh. Cracks and small holes marred its surface, but it remained intact—from base to tip. She was brushing an opaque liquid onto the tusk's tip from a quart-sized plastic container. She looked up as they came down the stairs and handed the consolidant to one of her graduate assistants.

Anita and Sam stepped into the basement and inched their way forward.

"Help yourselves to nitrile gloves from that box on the table," Fiona said. "You're welcome to touch it."

Sam slipped on gloves and dropped to his knees in front of the tusk. "My gosh, this is a beautiful specimen. It looks like the entire tusk is undamaged."

Fiona nodded. "It's in incredibly fine shape. We're thrilled."

Anita joined them. "How long is it?"

"Eight feet, eleven and a half inches," Fiona said. "Male mastodon tusks typically range from eight to ten feet. We think this specimen was probably from a young adult."

"How much does it weigh?" Sam asked.

"I can't give you an exact number yet," Fiona said, "but between eighty and a hundred pounds."

Anita reached out a gloved hand and ran it across the surface of the tusk.

"It's smoother than I thought it would be," she said. She rested her hand lightly on the highest part of the exposed arch. "This gives me chills. I'm touching something that's been here for over 10,000 years."

Sam brought his hand up to Anita's. "There's something majestic about this," he said. "I can see why these digs are so appealing."

Fiona smiled. "They're hours and hours of painstaking,

back-breaking work—often with no reward. But when you find something like this? It makes it all worthwhile." She looked over her shoulder at the students gathered behind her. They nodded in agreement.

"I promised Gordon I'd send him photos," Anita said.

"We've taken dozens," Fiona said. "I've already emailed them to Gordon—and to both of you."

"I haven't checked my email this afternoon. Thank you," Anita said.

"We'll finish applying the consolidant today and let it set before we begin casting. We should be finished by midafternoon. Once that's done, we'll leave early today to give it time to cure. Then next week …"

A cry from the group of students huddled behind her interrupted Fiona.

"There's something here!" one student called. He shone his flashlight onto something protruding from the floor. "It's either a rock—or more of this guy."

Fiona jumped to her feet, and the students scattered like Moses parting the Red Sea. She dropped to her knees, flipped her lighted magnifying glasses over her eyes, and bent close to the ground. Gingerly, she brushed dirt away from a jagged object protruding from the soil.

Everyone held their breath.

"It's a rib!" Fiona exclaimed, her voice electric with excitement.

She spun to Anita and Sam. "Want to see this?"

They walked gingerly around the tusk and joined her.

"Are you sure?" Sam asked, squinting at the protruding shape.

"I am," Fiona said. "Which means we won't be out of your hair next week, Anita—assuming you're still happy for us to keep excavating."

"Of course I am!" Anita cried. "This is what we've been hoping for."

"We'll remove the tusk by the middle of next week," Fiona said. "Then we'll begin searching for more of the skeleton. I need to call President Martin."

"I can't wait to tell Gordon," Anita said, rising to her feet.

"This is going to be big news in Westbury," Sam said. "Are you going to issue a press release?"

"We addressed that in our proposal," Fiona said. "The college will take care of it. But I'd like to wait until next week, after we've removed the tusk. I want to secure its safe removal and arrange for added security at the site before the world hears about this."

"Your proposal mentioned that excavation sites attract looters," Anita said. "But this site is inside a building with an alarm system. Do you really think we'll have problems?"

"Probably not," Fiona replied. "But I'd rather be safe than sorry." She raised her hand and snapped her fingers. "Everyone—we want to keep this additional discovery a secret until after we remove the tusk. I know this is exciting, and you want to tell your friends and family, but let's wait until next week." She looked at each student in turn. "Do I have your promise?"

They nodded in agreement, some more reluctantly than others.

Fiona turned back to Sam and Anita. "Other than Maggie and Gordon, we're keeping this between ourselves."

"Yes," they both said.

"And now," Fiona called out, "let's take care of this tusk—and get ready for an exciting week to come!"

CHAPTER 14

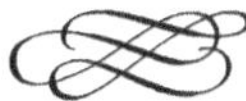

Colleen Connelly leaned against the wall in the hallway outside the president's suite. She was forty-five minutes early for her first day as President Martin's new administrative assistant. *It's best to be early for a new job,* her Irish grandmother had always said.

Colleen smoothed the skirt of the navy blue suit she'd bought over the weekend and tucked a lock of red hair behind her ear. If her name didn't disclose her Irish heritage, her ivory skin, blue eyes, and vibrant hair screamed it. She'd been born and raised in the United States, but living with her grandmother meant she could produce a credible Irish brogue whenever she wanted.

She glanced up and down the deserted hallway. The rich wood paneling and carved baseboards gave the space a solid, timeless air. The words *Office of the President* gleamed in gold lettering across the elaborate double doors. If only her late grandmother could see her now.

Colleen had graduated at the top of her high school class, all while holding down two part-time jobs to help support her younger siblings. Their grandmother had taken in all five children after their parents had died of cancer, only three months apart. The family had been left penniless. Her grandmother had done her best, but feeding five extra mouths was no small feat.

Colleen had earned several full-tuition scholarships, but she hadn't had the funds to cover living expenses. Instead, she'd worked full time and attended community college until her siblings grew up. Then, with her grandmother's blessing, she'd taken her savings and moved to Westbury. Highpointe College was the only school that had offered her another scholarship, now that she was in her thirties. Colleen worked a variety of odd jobs around town—waiting tables, cleaning houses, walking dogs, babysitting—while maintaining a straight-A average.

As soon as they posted the position of administrative assistant to the college president on the website, she'd applied. She lacked traditional office experience, aside from organizing a major fundraiser for her church's new sanctuary building. She'd included it on her application but didn't think it counted for much. Colleen had been sure she didn't stand a chance—but, as her grandmother had said, you always fail if you don't try.

She'd been so nervous the night before the first interview that she hadn't slept. She'd seen President Martin around campus, often sitting on benches, chatting with students. The woman seemed nice, but that hadn't made the interview any less intimidating.

When the call came for a second interview—the one where they offered her the job—Colleen hyperventilated. President Martin and Josh had sat across from her at the conference table, waiting for her response. She was so stunned she barely heard the details of the offer. The part about the job being hers, however, was perfectly clear. She'd accepted on the spot.

And now here she was, in new pumps and a clearance-rack suit, standing outside the president's office. She'd studied to be a teacher but had fallen in love with college administration. She'd graduated first in her class and been offered a scholarship for her master's degree. Now she was working for one of the most respected college presidents in the country. The years of sacrifice and hard work had paid off.

"Colleen!"

She turned to see Josh walking down the hall toward her.

"You're here early," he said. "I wanted to beat you in to the office this morning so I could get things ready for you. I meant to sneak in yesterday, but it didn't happen."

"Today's not only the first day back from spring break," she said with a smile, "but you're returning from your honeymoon, aren't you?"

Josh nodded and pulled a key from his pocket, unlocking the double doors and securing them open with doorstops. "Maggie likes an open-door policy when school's in session.

And yes, good memory. I got married a week ago Saturday. We cut our honeymoon short because we bought a house."

"My goodness—that's a lot in one week," she said.

"Tell me about it." He dropped his satchel behind his desk. "We won't close for another four weeks, but the owners are letting us take possession early. My wife decided we should paint the interior before we move in."

"That makes sense," Colleen said. "Much easier to paint when it's empty."

"Exactly. But still a lot of work. We started painting this weekend and didn't make a dent in it. Sunday—that's my wife—Sunday Sloan. Have you met her?"

Colleen shook her head. "No."

"She's a librarian at Highpointe. Rare books. She's the one Nigel Blythe tried to kill in the library."

"Oh!" Colleen snapped her fingers. "That was her?"

"The very one," Josh said. "Almost everyone in town knows about that."

"It was in the news for weeks. The whole thing was shocking," Colleen added.

Josh walked to the coffee bar and opened a drawer. "What would you like? It's a fancy cup-at-a-time machine. We've got at least half a dozen choices."

Colleen selected a pod, popped it into the machine, and placed a china mug with the Highpointe logo beneath the spout. The machine rumbled to life.

"So," Josh continued, "we're painting the house, packing, moving, and I'm also finishing coursework for my master's degree."

"That's even more than I thought. I'm happy to work extra here to help lighten your load. I promise I'm a fast learner," she added, hoping she sounded confident.

"Maggie and I both know you'll hit the ground running," Josh said.

She stepped aside to let him make his coffee. "Throw anything at me, and I'll take care of it."

"I'm glad to hear that," he replied. "Because Maggie and I are both leaving the office this morning to attend the groundbreaking for Forever Guides."

"I heard about that on the radio," she said. "We're going to have a seeing-eye dog training facility in Westbury. I think that's very cool."

"Me too. I'll be the director of education at Forever Guides when it's up and running. Until then, I'll manage Forever Friends, which is owned by the same people and right next door."

"That sounds like a fabulous career move," Colleen said. "Congratulations."

"Thanks." He smiled. "So—after I graduate, I'll also be starting a new job."

She patted his arm. "It all sounds brilliant to me."

He grabbed his mug of coffee. "Let's get you started." He led her to the desk. "You'll sort Maggie's email into three folders: Immediate Attention, Review This Week, and Review on a Slow Day. Those are the actual folder names."

"Makes perfect sense," she said.

"Eventually, you'll be able to reply to some of the emails on your own. Maggie delegates what she thinks you can handle, and she's very supportive. She's had my back from day one—you'll find she does the same for you."

He motioned for Colleen to sit in the desk chair and pulled one for himself from the waiting area, and they put their heads together. By the time Maggie walked in thirty minutes later, Colleen was making quick work of her inbox.

Maggie welcomed her with a warm handshake. "Let's have lunch this week so we can become better acquainted."

"Thank you, President Martin," Colleen said.

"First order of business—it's Maggie, not President Martin."

"Maggie, then," Colleen replied, smiling.

"I want to hear about your week off," Maggie said to Josh. "Judy told me your news at church yesterday. Congratulations! I've got a call with Fiona in five minutes, so I need to grab my coffee and head into my office."

"Really?" Josh asked. "I don't see the call on your calendar."

"Sorry—we set it up Friday afternoon, and I forgot to add it." She turned to Colleen. "I'm bad about that—scheduling myself and not putting it on the calendar. You have my permission to call me out on it. You need to know what I've got going on."

She crossed to the coffeemaker. "Anyway, Josh and I are leaving shortly for the groundbreaking. Carry on with what you're doing, and we'll catch up later."

CHAPTER 15

Frank Haynes walked from his office at Forever Friends to the reception area. The space buzzed with activity this Monday morning. Loretta and Marissa were transferring the dog-shaped cookies they'd spent the prior afternoon baking at Joan's house—with the assistance of Joan and Gloria—onto trays at the refreshment table. Gloria was removing cocktail napkins, decorated with drawings of happy dog faces, from their cellophane packaging.

Bonnie and Branson, strapped into their double stroller, began to kick their legs and fuss as soon as they saw their father. Nicole stood in front of them, waving a puppet to distract them.

Joan came through the front door holding a stack of plastic boxes containing cookies. "In case we run out of those and need reinforcements," she told Loretta. "There are already people out there, and the groundbreaking doesn't start for another twenty minutes."

"This all looks great, ladies," Frank said. "I'd better get David and head over there. Has anyone seen him?"

"He's with Sean in the kennels," Loretta said without looking away from her task.

The twins increased the decibel of their protest as Frank walked past them on his way to find David.

Loretta straightened and took a step back. "Frank," she called to him. "Will the three of you take the twins with you? They'll be happier outside."

Frank turned back. "David and I are part of the program. We can't watch them."

"We'll be there by the time it starts," Loretta said. "Besides, you'll have Sean with you. You'll be fine." She returned her attention to the reception table.

"Sure. I'll grab David," Frank mumbled and continued to the kennels.

David Wheeler and Sean were walking along the row of rescue dogs, scratching noses and rubbing ears through the metal grates.

"We'd better get over there," Frank said, joining them. "The podium is set up. We should test the microphone for the speeches we'll be making."

David stopped short. "What do you mean 'we'? I'm not making a speech. I'm just here to watch."

"Forever Guides was your brainchild," Frank said. "Don't you want to say something to the crowd that supported your dream?"

"Definitely not," David said. "I hate public speaking."

"Okay," Frank said, "The mayor and I will do all the talking." He turned to Sean. "Will you help your mother finish whatever she's doing and make sure she's on time for the groundbreaking?"

The boy nodded and headed for the refreshment table.

Frank and David collected the stroller and pushed it toward the group congregating in the middle of the vacant lot that would soon become home to Forever Guides. Bonnie and Branson settled down as the stroller bumped across the uneven terrain.

"Are you excited about today?" Frank asked.

"I sure am," David replied. "Sometimes I can't believe it's really happening. I need to thank Gordon Mortimer again. We're not supposed to know he's our benefactor, but it's the worst-kept secret in town. I'm disappointed he won't be here today."

"Gordon is, too," Frank said. "He called me over the weekend to tell me he had an urgent business trip to London and can't get back in time. He plans to be in Westbury on Wednesday afternoon, though."

"I go back to the Guide Dog Center tomorrow," David said. "We're shorthanded, and I could only get two days off. That's why I flew home for the groundbreaking—it's too far to drive."

Frank wheeled the stroller through the crowd and parked it close to the podium. A familiar figure popped out of the crowd and sprinted toward the babies. Grace Acosta dropped to her knees and opened her arms to them, leaning in to plant a kiss on Branson's cheek and then Bonnie's. "Look how big you are," she said in a singsong voice. "I haven't babysat you since right after Christmas."

The twins erupted into laughter and flung out their arms to her, asking to be picked up. "I can't, you guys. I'm working," she replied, knowing as she said it that they didn't understand.

She stood and turned toward Frank. "School's almost out. I have time to babysit this summer, if you and …" Her words froze on her lips when she saw David standing next to Frank.

The former high school sweethearts stared at each other. "Hi, David." Grace broke the silence. "I wondered if you'd come home for the groundbreaking."

David nodded. He opened his mouth to speak, but couldn't force out the words.

Frank glanced between them. "Nice to see you, Grace. Bonnie and Branson clearly remember—and miss—you. I'll tell Loretta. I'm sure she'll call you."

"Great. I'll look forward to spending time with these two," she said, casting a fond glance at the twins.

Frank looked at David, who remained mute. "Thanks for coming to the groundbreaking," he said to Grace. "Did I hear you say that you're working?"

Grace nodded. "I'm a reporter for the Highpointe newspaper," she said. "I cover stories about Westbury and the surrounding area. Our goal is to make students feel connected to Westbury, so they consider remaining here when they graduate. We want to retain the talent that we develop at Highpointe."

"That's a terrific idea," Frank said. "Who came up with that?"

"I'll bet Grace did." David found his voice. "She's always been smart about things like that."

Grace trained her thousand-watt smile on David. "That's so nice of you."

David looked like a stagehand suddenly caught in the spotlight.

Frank pointed to Alex Scanlon and his partner, Mark Benson, as they made their way from their car to the podium. "We're about to start," he said to Grace. "I'll be sure to let Loretta know you're available this summer."

Grace slipped into the crowd as more people arrived.

The four men exchanged greetings. Frank and Alex stepped to one side to review the program one last time.

Loretta and the big kids stepped into place by the stroller. David edged away from the podium to join them. Loretta swept him into a hug. "I'm so happy to see you!"

"Where's Dodger?" Nicole asked.

"I'm only here for a couple of days," David replied, "so I left him in California. My landlord has taken him in. I'm sure Dodger's having the time of his life with Jack and his dog. Dodger and Dory are besties now." David glanced at the little girl. Nicole looked crestfallen.

"Can you come over to spend time with us?" Nicole asked. "You need to see Daisy, too. She's getting fantastic at agility. Sean can show you."

"I wish I could," David said, "but I fly out in the morning, and I promised my mom I'd spend this evening with her." Nicole nodded sullenly.

A van from the local television news station parked at the curb. A well-dressed reporter and a camera operator joined the crowd and positioned themselves at an optimal viewing angle.

Maggie and Josh were next to arrive, followed immediately by John, Anita, Sam and Joan, Glenn and Gloria, and Tim. The staff of Forever Friends walked over just before the ceremony started. A reporter from the Westbury Gazette slipped into place as Frank approached the podium.

"Thank you all for coming out this morning," Frank said into the microphone.

"Before I introduce Mayor Scanlon for his official remarks, I need to bring someone else to stand with us at the podium." He pointed to David.

David's facial expression morphed from happy and excited to deer-in-the-headlights.

"Forever Guides would not be happening without the vision and heart of one very special member of our community: David Wheeler." He motioned for David to join them. "Get up here and take your rightful place."

The crowd clapped. Josh whistled between his teeth. David reluctantly made his way to the podium and stood next to Frank, facing the crowd.

Frank put an arm around David's shoulder. "And now I'll turn this over to Mayor Alex Scanlon." Frank stepped back.

David scanned the crowd, searching for the girlfriend

he'd thought of every day for months. He had convinced himself of the wisdom of their breakup. They were kids, going to distant colleges, and needed to date other people. They were too young to get serious. High school romances didn't survive years of separation. He sighed heavily. Now that he'd seen Grace again, and his heart had been saturated with joy the moment she'd smiled at him, he knew it was all a lie. Grace Acosta was the one for him. His eyes found her, scribbling madly on a spiral-bound notebook, and they never left her.

Alex stepped to the microphone. "We've gathered this morning to celebrate the beginning of Forever Guides. This isn't just a new building—it's a dream taking shape, a vision coming to life, and a lot of love and effort finally paying off."

"Forever Guides will be a place where lives are changed. The school will breed, raise, and train guide dogs, and match them with visually impaired individuals. These guide dog/dog handler partnerships open up new worlds of independence and confidence for the visually impaired. That's powerful stuff. And it's happening right here in our community."

"Westbury owes a huge thank you to everyone who made this possible—to David Wheeler, whose dream ignited this project, to the founders like Frank Haynes, to the donors, and to the volunteers behind the scenes who've worked so hard to get us to this moment. Be very proud of what you've brought into reality."

"This place will do amazing things. It'll help people live more fully. It's going to create lifelong partnerships. And it'll remind all of us what's possible when a community comes together around something that really matters."

"Westbury is proud to be the home of Forever Guides."

He reached for the shovel leaning against the podium and held it out to Frank. Frank stepped back and pressed David forward to accept it.

"Let's break ground and get to work!" Alex concluded.

Applause erupted again. David grasped the shovel with a glazed look in his eyes and stepped to a patch of dirt in front of the podium. He stood, the shovel poised to go into the ground.

"Put it into the ground and dig up some dirt," Glenn said in a stage whisper.

David shook his head like he was rousing himself from a deep sleep and turned the first spade of dirt.

"Do we have time to stop by Forever Friends for refreshments?" Josh turned to Maggie as the crowd dispersed.

"Call Colleen and see how she's doing," Maggie replied. "If everything's under control at the office, I'd like to. Joan, Gloria, and Loretta and her older girls spent yesterday afternoon baking dog-shaped sugar cookies. I want to congratulate them—and snag one of those cookies." She rose on her tiptoes and leaned to look around Josh.

"Alex!" she called, raising her hand over her head and waving.

Alex offered a small wave in return, then spun on his heel and made a beeline for his car.

"Wait!" Maggie called after him. She stepped around Josh. "I'll catch up with you at the reception," she added over her shoulder, hurrying to follow Alex. She called to him again, raising her voice to be sure he heard her.

He turned and smiled. "Hey, Maggie."

"Aren't you going to the reception?" she asked.

He shook his head. "I have to get back to Town Hall."

Maggie waited for him to elaborate, but he remained silent as he resumed walking to his car.

"Just a minute," she said. "We need to talk."

He stopped and turned to face her.

"If you haven't heard already, I wanted you to know that Fiona's team uncovered an additional bone from the mastodon in Anita's basement."

His eyebrows shot up. "I hadn't heard that."

"They found it on Friday," she said. "Fiona asked that we hold the press release about it until the tusk has been safely moved to the lab at the college. That should happen tomorrow or Wednesday at the latest. As soon as the tusk is secure at Highpointe, we'll issue a press release."

"Mum's the word," Alex replied. "Thank you for telling me." He started walking to his car again.

Maggie fell into step beside him. "What do you think about this mastodon?" she asked. "Does Westbury have any interest in the archaeological find?"

Alex shrugged. "Why would we? It's on private property."

"Within the town," Maggie said. "If I were still mayor, I'd be interested in it."

They reached his car.

"Thanks for the tip," Alex said. "I'll think about it." He opened his door and slipped behind the wheel. "Say hi to John for me. I'm sorry we haven't seen more of you guys—we've been busy."

Marc, who had been trailing behind them, gave Maggie a rueful smile and climbed into the passenger seat. Alex pulled away from the curb, leaving Maggie on the sidewalk, staring after them.

MAGGIE SWIVELED to see John loping across the vacant lot toward her.

"Looks like you and Alex were disagreeing about something," he said when he caught up with her.

"Why do you say that?" Maggie asked.

"Body language," he replied. "Stiff bodies and no hugs. That's unusual for the two of you. What's up?"

Maggie bit her lip. "I don't know. It's probably nothing. I don't want to get into it right now—we can talk tonight."

"You're sure?" John asked.

Maggie nodded. "I'm sure. You need to get back to the Animal Hospital."

John checked his watch. "I'll be late as it is." He leaned in and kissed her cheek. "See you tonight, and you can tell me everything."

She nodded, and they turned to go their separate ways.

Maggie entered Forever Friends and wove her way through the crowd to the refreshment table. In the center sat a tray of assorted cookies. Only three of the decorated sugar cookies her friends had made the day before remained. She picked up a cocktail napkin, grabbed a dog-shaped cookie, and joined Anita, who was standing along the wall to the right of the door.

"You've got an exciting week ahead of you, with the tusk removal and the additional excavation," Maggie said.

Anita shrugged.

"Are you disappointed Gordon wasn't here?"

"Of course," Anita said, "but I understand—he has important business overseas. I can't expect him to be in two places at once."

"Exactly," Maggie said, biting the tail off her cookie. She studied Anita. "Something else is bothering you. Are you having second thoughts about the excavation?"

"No—nothing of the kind. I'm thrilled about that."

"Then what?" Maggie pressed.

"It's Gordon. Or rather, Gordon and me," Anita admitted. "We've been texting multiple times each day and talking every night at bedtime for months—but we've barely spoken since he went back to New York after Sunday and Josh's wedding."

"Did something happen that day?" Maggie asked.

"No. We had a wonderful time. He's been fully engaged in every aspect of the excavation and the museum, too. I texted him when they uncovered the tusk, and again when they found what they think is a rib bone." She turned to meet Maggie's eyes. "He hearted my texts and that's it. He hasn't called either."

"That doesn't sound like him," Maggie said. "He has to be extremely busy. That must be why he didn't come for the groundbreaking."

"He missed today because he had a last-minute business trip to London."

"I wondered why he wasn't here. Now it makes sense that you haven't heard from him. He's busy, and you're dealing with a big time difference."

"That's what I keep telling myself," Anita said, "but I worry something's wrong—that I've offended him and he's mad at me."

"Gordon isn't the type to stalk off in a huff," Maggie reassured her. "If anything were wrong, I'm sure he'd say something to you."

"You honestly think so?" Anita asked.

"Definitely," Maggie replied.

"He also texted me to say he wouldn't be here today for the groundbreaking," Anita continued, "but I understand he called Frank. I mean, if he had time to call Frank, why didn't he call me?"

"There are plenty of explanations for that," Maggie said. "None of them have anything to do with him losing interest in you." She put a hand on her friend's shoulder. "I think you're making yourself miserable over nothing. When will you see him again?"

"Wednesday afternoon," Anita replied.

"My advice is to put your worries and suspicions aside and wait until you see him."

Anita forced a smile that didn't quite reach her eyes. "That's sound advice. I'll do my best to take it."

Maggie took another bite of her cookie and focused her attention on the people milling around in front of them.

Joan and Sam Torres stopped to say hello on their way out. "I'm glad you got one of the cookies we made," Joan said. "Marissa and Nicole did the decorating, so, if you see them, be sure to compliment them."

"Will do," Maggie said. "They're beautiful."

Sam looked from Anita to Maggie and back again. "The two of you look like you lost the winning lottery ticket. What's wrong?"

Maggie and Anita glanced at each other, then turned back to him.

"Everything's fine," Maggie said.

"Couldn't be better," Anita added.

"If you say so," Sam said, glancing between them as he followed his wife out the door.

CHAPTER 16

Alistair

The door into the house from the garage shut a little more firmly than usual. I was sure of it. Roman and Eve jumped from their beds by the hearth and raced to the kitchen. I followed at a more decorous pace.

The clacking of high heels told me our mistress was home. She set the takeout bags on the kitchen counter, but didn't stop to retrieve a treat for my friends from the canister on the counter. Her pace was brisk, and we intersected at the base of the staircase. She bounded up the steps to her room without a backward glance at the dogs, who were hanging back, looking from her to the kitchen. They were trying to remind her that she had forgotten their treats, but she ignored them.

Maggie was in a mood. That much was certain.

I floated toward the stairs just as the kitchen door opened

again. The dogs raced to greet John, who walked straight to the treat container. Roman and Eve sat at his feet, their eyes locked on his hand. He tossed them each a treat, which they caught in midair. I was pleased that he had rectified this breach of household routine. In my day as butler, everything had run on time. My mantra was that an efficient household was a happy household.

"Where's your mommy?" John asked the dogs. They raised their eyes to him, wagging their tails rapidly enough to create a draft. "Upstairs? Let's go find her."

John led the way, and the three of us followed him to the bedroom. Maggie had changed into a T-shirt and a pair of form-fitting pants. Athleisure, I believe they call it. Indecent was a better term. Those pants wouldn't have passed for knickers in my day.

"You're home," John said, crossing the room and taking her into his arms. "Are we eating in or going out?"

"Definitely staying in," Maggie said. "I stopped at Pete's on the way home and picked up the daily special."

"It's Monday, so it must be meatloaf," John said. "That's one of my favorites."

Maggie brushed his cheek with a kiss. "You say that about every daily special."

"What can I say?" He shrugged. "I'm not a picky eater."

"That's one of the many things I love about you," Maggie said. "You've never complained about my cooking."

"That's because you're a great cook," John said, looking at her intently. "Is everything okay, sweetheart?"

She took a deep breath, then blew it out with a sigh. "I'm upset with Alex," she said, stepping back.

"Why?"

"It's complicated," she said. "Let's talk about it while we eat. That's why I picked up takeout—I want your full attention without interruption."

His eyebrows shot up. "Sounds serious. I'll change and be right down."

Maggie headed for the stairs, and I tailed her. Alex was like a second son to her. After an arson fire had destroyed their home, he and Marc stayed with us at Rosemont. And Alex had recuperated here after his grievous injuries from his car accident. I'd never heard a cross word between him and Maggie. Whatever was going on, I needed to know.

She removed two take-out boxes from the brown carrier bag. Opening one, she touched the contents with her fingertip. "Needs to be warmed up," she said, glancing at the dogs. She popped the container into the contraption on the counter that spun things around on a plate and dinged when done.

Maggie opened the silverware drawer and retrieved knives and forks. She stopped at the treat jar. "*Oh my gosh,*" she said, turning to Roman and Eve. "I forgot your treats. Mommy's sorry." She quickly set the table, returned to the jar, and gave each dog two treats.

The contraption dinged, and Maggie switched out the containers.

John returned, now in jeans and a T-shirt, and poured

them each a glass of iced tea. Maggie set one container holding a warmed-up meal at each place setting.

"Do you want me to get plates? We never eat out of the containers," he said.

"You can if you want, but this is fine," Maggie replied.

His eyes widened. Our Maggie never ate out of take-out boxes. John and I were both alarmed by this abandonment of standards.

John sat. "I'm ready to listen whenever you're ready to tell me."

Maggie took a sip of tea. "I told you about my meeting with Fiona and Anita last week?"

John nodded. "You were annoyed that Alex asked Fiona if she'd be interested in managing a natural history museum in Westbury."

Maggie nodded.

"A natural history museum that doesn't exist," John said. "So you really had nothing to worry about. Has something changed?"

"That's just it," Maggie said. "Fiona called last Friday to tell me they found a rib bone from the mastodon."

"That's exciting," John said. "Why didn't you tell me?"

"I should've," Maggie admitted. "Fiona asked me not to tell anyone until they remove the tusk in the next day or two. We'll put out a press release after that. She's worried that once word gets out, a crowd will gather outside Stitches in Time and make their work harder. I'm sorry. I know you wouldn't have leaked it."

"Of course not. But that's okay. I understand—you were keeping your word. You're trustworthy."

A faint smile crossed her lips. "Now that they've found part of the skeleton, this museum district idea of Alex's isn't so abstract anymore."

"You said you thought the district was a terrific idea," John said.

"It is," Maggie replied. "I just don't like the idea of Alex poaching my employee without even contacting me first."

"You don't own Fiona," John said gently. "If she's as good as you say she is, she probably gets other employment offers on a regular basis. Her leaving Highpointe is always a possibility."

Maggie leaned back and stared at him.

"Employees I value leave all the time," John said. "Juan—my best tech—is quitting at the end of the summer to go to vet school. I'm happy for him."

"I'm not mad at Fiona," Maggie said, her words clipped. "My beef is with Alex. I think it's inappropriate for him to sniff around her without mentioning it first."

"Maybe he hasn't had a chance," John said. "You know how busy he is."

"That's why I'm upset—he had a chance this morning."

"Did you talk to him at the reception?"

"I tried. He hightailed it out as soon as the groundbreaking was over. I had to run after him, calling his name. I swear he heard me and wanted to get away."

"Why would he do that?" John asked.

"Because he's feeling guilty for betraying me."

John reached for her hand. She pulled it back.

My head swiveled between them, as if I were watching a tennis match.

"When you were mayor, you said you had to put the town's best interests first," John reminded her. "If the citizens of Westbury thought it was appropriate to offer a job to a highly qualified person like Fiona—even if they are currently working for a former mayor—what would they expect our current mayor to do?"

Maggie's eyes narrowed.

"They wouldn't say, 'Don't do it, Alex, because you might annoy Maggie.'"

Maggie crumpled her napkin and tossed it into her empty container, then stalked to the trash.

"I don't mean to upset you," John said, following her. "But you need to think about this from a broader perspective."

"You don't know the whole story," Maggie said. "When I told him about the rib bone, I asked if the town had any interest in the mastodon. He said no because it was on private property. I told him, if *I* were still mayor, I'd be interested in this remarkable find. All he said was, 'I'll have to think about it.'"

"Okay," John said.

"Which means he lied to me." Her voice rose in volume. "He doesn't need to think about it. He's already dreamed up this museum district and is attempting to hire Fiona. It hurts that Alex lied to me, considering our history."

"I think you're jumping to conclusions," John said. "He could feel torn between Westbury's interests and yours."

Maggie stepped around him and put her glass in the dishwasher. "I'm going upstairs."

"Want to watch some TV?"

"I think I'll read." She walked away.

I'd never seen them fight before, and I disliked discord in my home. My mind was reeling. I loved Maggie, but I was Team John on this issue.

Roman followed John, while Eve and I made our way upstairs to Maggie.

CHAPTER 17

Jackie Wheeler opened her front door early the next morning and blinked in surprise.

"Glenn?"

"Morning, Jackie." His voice was warm, steady. "I'm here to pick up David for breakfast. Frank and I worked it out with him yesterday—we haven't seen much of him lately and wanted to catch up. You're not heading to the airport until ten, right? Plenty of time for Pete's pancakes."

"He didn't mention it." She stepped back, holding the door wide. "Come in."

Glenn crossed the threshold, his sneakers quiet on the floor. "You sure it's okay? We'll have him back well before you need to go."

"Please," Jackie said with a sigh of relief. "It's more than okay. David's been in a blue funk since the groundbreaking.

Every time I ask what's wrong, he just mutters 'nothing.' But it's not nothing. Maybe you can get through to him."

Glenn's mouth curved into a knowing half-smile. "I have an idea what's eating at him."

Jackie's shoulders loosened. "I hope so. You and Frank have been like the father and grandfather he never had." Her voice wavered on father.

Glenn reached out, his hand resting on her shoulder with quiet reassurance. "Frank and I both love that boy like he's our own. Don't worry. Leave this to us."

She leaned into his touch for the briefest moment, then straightened. "I'll get him. He's been sulking in his room."

Moments later, David appeared, trailing behind her. His clothes looked pressed, and his hair was neatly combed, but his eyes—shadowed and tired—betrayed him.

Glenn's smile was steady. "Hungry? Pete's still serves the best pancakes in town."

David shrugged, forcing the faintest grin.

"We'll have him back by ten," Glenn promised, guiding him toward the car.

From the doorway, Jackie watched them go. She hugged her arms around herself, silently praying that David would let the walls down and tell these men—who loved him like their own—what was really wrong.

THE SMELL OF COFFEE, bacon, and fresh cinnamon rolls

spilled onto the sidewalk in front of Pete's Bistro. David opened the door for Glenn, and they stepped inside.

Frank waved from a corner booth. Glenn nodded to the hostess as they passed her stand.

"He's waiting for you in your usual spot," she said. "Your server will be right over with coffee."

David slid into the booth, eyes scanning the familiar chaos of the morning rush. "I'd forgotten how great this place is," he said, though his voice lacked its usual spark. "I guess I do miss Westbury."

The server appeared with a coffeepot. "You two want your usuals?"

"Of course," Frank said.

She poured coffee all around. "How about you, young man—want to see a menu?"

David shook his head. "I already know what I want—a chorizo omelet and a large stack of blueberry pancakes."

"You got it," she said, moving off toward the kitchen.

Glenn studied him over the rim of his cup. "You didn't say a word on the drive over here. What's on your mind?"

David stirred sugar into his coffee, his gaze fixed on the swirling liquid. "Guess I'm just tired."

"Tired, huh?" Frank said. "That's not what your mom thinks. She says you've been walking around like somebody canceled Christmas."

"Between the two of us," Glenn said, "we've got over a hundred years of spotting when somebody's holding something in. And you, my friend, are holding something in."

David gave a faint shrug. "Like I said—I miss Westbury."

Frank tore open a sweetener packet, shaking his head. "You've been in California long enough that I don't think this is homesickness. And you know me—I'll keep asking until you spill it just to shut me up."

The server returned with steaming plates, two with bacon and all three with towering stacks of pancakes, each crowned with a melting slab of butter.

David picked up his fork. "You guys are worse than my mom."

"We'll take that as a compliment," Glenn said.

Frank leaned in slightly. "Whatever it is, you don't have to carry it alone. You know I learned that the hard way—when I wouldn't forgive myself for the mistakes I made."

David looked up, caught in Frank's steady gaze.

"You got through to me, David," Frank went on. "You made me see I was worthy of the family I love so much. Without your love and support, I might not still be married to Loretta, or have Bonnie and Branson in my life." His voice thickened. "You were there for me, and I'm here for you."

"Both of us are," Glenn added.

David's fork hovered over his plate. "I know." He hesitated, chewing his lower lip. "It's … complicated."

Glenn's brow lifted. "May I hazard a guess?"

David glanced up warily. "Sure."

"I agree with Frank—this isn't about homesickness. I'm guessing …" Glenn pointed at him, circling his finger slowly, "… this is about a woman."

David dropped his fork and leaned back.

"Bull's-eye," Frank said, slapping the table with his open palm. "It's Grace Acosta, isn't it? I should have known. When you saw her at the groundbreaking yesterday, you turned into a tongue-tied, bumbling idiot."

"Thanks a lot," David muttered.

"I saw that exchange too," Glenn said. "You weren't a bumbling idiot—you were simply blindsided."

"I was," David admitted. "I didn't expect to see her there. We haven't talked for months."

"You told me you both agreed to date other people when you left for California and she started college," Glenn said. "You felt you were too young to make a serious commitment."

David nodded, his expression shadowed.

"And you told me, if it was meant to be, you'd find each other later," Glenn concluded.

"That's just it," David said. "All my feelings resurfaced when I saw her yesterday. I don't want to date anyone else. Grace is the one for me."

"Did you tell her that?" Frank asked.

David shook his head. "Of course not. I saw her at the reception at Forever Friends. She was busy talking to other people, and, by the time I worked up the nerve to find her, she'd already left."

"And now you're headed back to California," Frank said.

David nodded, looking more deflated than when they'd walked in.

"You kids know how to stay in constant communication," Glenn said. "Call her, text her, WhatsApp her—whatever you use."

"Yeah," David scoffed, "only to find out she's got a boyfriend. I wanted to talk to her here—see if she's seeing anyone."

"So ask her over the phone or by text," Frank said. "What's the big deal?"

"I'll look like an idiot—like a bumbling idiot, as you said."

"Sometimes you've got to keep pressing your point," Glenn said. "Gloria and I were friends. When I wanted more, she said no because she's seven years older than me and thought we were too old for romance. I kept our friendship alive, but left notes and little gifts at her door every day until she changed her mind. We've been married for years now, happy as clams. I risked the heartbreak of her rejection by going for the happiness we currently enjoy."

"I'll make you a deal," Frank said. "Loretta called Grace last night after we got home from the groundbreaking. She's babysitting for us on Saturday night. Loretta will find out if she's dating anyone and if she still has feelings for you."

"I don't want Grace to think I put Loretta up to it," David said.

"No worries, son," Glenn said. "These women are masters of subtle interrogation."

"Loretta and I will call you Sunday," Frank added. "If she's not in love with someone else, then you make your move."

David cracked his first genuine smile of the morning. "Okay. I can do that. Thanks—both of you."

Glenn clapped him on the back. "Don't ever forget we're here for you, son." He checked his watch. "We've got ten minutes before we need to head back to your house—and a lot of food to eat."

Forks flew as the three men attacked their breakfasts with singular focus.

CHAPTER 18

Gordon and Tim rushed through the lobby toward the bank of elevators. Gordon surged ahead, trying to slip inside before the doors closed, but they shut in his face. He stabbed the up button three times in quick succession.

"You're in a hurry," Tim commented.

"Sorry," Gordon said. "I promised Anita I'd meet her at Stitches in Time at three. Apparently, Fiona has another surprise in store, and Anita wants me there for the big reveal." He hesitated, then added, "I want to be there for the big reveal, too."

"I've already looked at the paperwork," Tim said. "Everything's in order. All you have to do is sign, and you'll be on your way. The lawyers have everything ready for you."

The elevator pinged, and the doors opened at last.

Gordon waited impatiently for the occupants to exit, then flung himself inside.

"The law firm's on the fourth floor," Tim supplied, and Gordon punched the button. They ascended in silence.

The receptionist greeted them with a smile. "Mr. Gray asked that I show you to the conference room." She led them down a short hall into a wood-paneled room lined with bookcases. A long conference table dominated the space. Three neat stacks of documents were arranged at one end. "Can I get you coffee? There's bottled water on the credenza."

Both men shook their heads.

"Mr. Gray will be right in," she said, closing the door. But Mr. Gray was not right in. Ten minutes passed. Then twenty.

"I'm going to be late for my meeting with Anita," Gordon muttered.

"She knows meetings like this can run long," Tim said. "She'll understand."

"That's just it." Gordon exhaled. "She doesn't know I'm here."

Tim tilted his head, eyes narrowing. "Anita doesn't know you're signing your house papers this afternoon?"

"She doesn't even know I'm buying a place in Westbury. I want it to be a surprise," Gordon said.

"Okaaay …" Tim drew the word out.

"It's a long story," Gordon said, looking uncharacteristically flustered. "As I've said, it's important that we keep this purchase quiet."

"I understand," Tim replied. "But I didn't think that meant

keeping it a secret from Anita, too. Honestly, I'm a little surprised she isn't here—especially since you're buying that dilapidated mansion near the square that we both know she loves."

"The lawyers won't say anything, will they?" Gordon asked. "That's why I'm buying it through an LLC. I don't want my name attached until ..." He trailed off, color creeping from his collar to the top of his head. "... until I'm ready for everyone to know."

"They won't say a word," Tim said. "That house has sat vacant behind the square for decades—no one even notices it anymore. I assume you're going to renovate?"

"Yes. It has to be taken down to the studs," Gordon said.

"Well, once construction crews arrive, the whole town will be buzzing. Speculation about the new owner will be everywhere."

"By then," Gordon said quietly, "I should know."

Tim waited for him to elaborate, but Gordon remained silent. The grandfather clock in the corner ticked away the minutes.

Gordon's phone buzzed in his pocket. Anita. He checked his watch—it was past three. He hesitated, then swiped to answer.

"Hi, sweetheart," Anita said. "Sam and I are with Fiona for the next great reveal. I'm calling to see how far out you are. We're happy to wait. I assume you got delayed on the highway from the airport."

"Yes, darling. I'm so sorry," Gordon said, surprised at how easily the lie rolled off his tongue. "There's a terrible pile-up just west of the airport. We haven't moved an inch in twenty minutes."

"That's horrible," Anita said. "I hate being stuck in traffic like that—not knowing how long it'll be. Feels almost claustrophobic. What should I tell Fiona?"

"You'd best go ahead without me," Gordon said. "I don't want to hold you up, and I know she needs to leave the site in an hour."

"I hate that you're going to miss the fun. These discoveries really are special."

"I do, too. Will you take me there tonight after dinner to show me?"

"Sure. Call when you get into town, okay?"

"Will do."

"And drive carefully, Gordon. I want you here in one piece."

He tapped the screen to end the call and slid the phone back into his pocket. Sinking into his chair, he turned to Tim. "I just lied to Anita."

"It was only a little white lie," Tim replied in a consoling tone. "Once the attorney gets here, we'll breeze through the paperwork and get you on your way."

"Thanks, Tim," Gordon replied. "I know it's hard to keep something a secret in Westbury, but I'm going to try."

CHAPTER 19

Gordon signed the final document and placed it squarely atop the stack of papers. He pushed back from the conference table and rose, leaning forward with his hand outstretched. "Thank you for your time—"

"We're not quite done," the attorney interrupted. "I have the keys and some information about utility hookups for you. Unfortunately, I left them in my office. I'll be right back." He hurried out.

Gordon sighed in frustration and checked his watch. "If I leave right now, I might still catch Anita at Stitches in Time. I don't have a moment to spare."

"I'll stay and collect the keys," Tim said. "And anything else Gray brings back. I'll get them to you tomorrow."

"You're sure?" Gordon asked, already edging toward the door.

"Positive. Get out of here."

"Thanks, Tim." Gordon was halfway into the hall before the words left his mouth. On the elevator ride down, he composed a quick text to Anita: *I'll be at museum in under ten minutes.*

In the parking garage, his phone pinged. Sliding into the driver's seat, he opened her reply: *Was just locking up. Very exciting find. Everyone else is gone. I'll wait here to show you.*

He backed out and made the short drive to the museum as quickly as he dared.

Anita was outside, leaning against the building, her face tilted toward the sky. When she spotted him, her smile shot straight through him like sunlight breaching a storm cloud. He crossed the sidewalk in three long strides and pulled her into his arms.

She accepted his kiss but shrank back. "Gordon—we're on a public street. We're not teenagers."

"I can't help it," he protested. "When you smile at me like that, I *feel* like a teenager."

She took his hand and led him inside, shutting the door behind them. They finished their kiss in the quiet of the empty museum.

"I didn't think I could last much longer without one of those," Gordon murmured. "Now—show me what's got you so excited in that basement."

Anita led him down the narrow stairs and pointed to a thirteen-foot-long trough, a foot wide and eighteen inches deep. "That's where the tusk was. Here—take this." She handed him a flashlight and took one for herself.

"The rib is over here." She led him to a curved length of bone, uncovered to a depth of two feet. "Fiona says ribs can be as long as five feet, depending on their position."

"How many do mastodons have?"

"Seventeen pairs—thirty-four total."

Gordon crouched, sweeping his light along the curve of the bone.

"They haven't started applying consolidant yet," Anita said. "It'll take another couple of days to fully excavate."

"That's quite a find," Gordon said, standing.

"That's not what Fiona was most excited to show us." Anita took his hand and led him a few feet farther, stopping at a marked-off quadrant where an eight-inch-deep square had been carefully dug. The beam of her flashlight revealed a smooth gray mound at its center.

Gordon raised his eyebrows.

"That," Anita said, "is the top of this creature's skull."

He dropped to his knees and held the flashlight beam steady.

"Fiona says it's only a small portion," Anita continued. "They'll need a week or more to uncover the rest."

"How big are mastodon skulls?"

"Three and a half to four feet long and three feet wide. They weigh several hundred pounds." Anita knelt beside him. They regarded the unremarkable-looking hump of bone with the reverence of people who knew its significance.

"This is incredible," Gordon said. "I wish I'd been here for the discovery."

"It doesn't look like much right now, but when Fiona and her crew showed us ... it was like they were presenting the crown jewels. Their enthusiasm is contagious."

"I imagine it is." Although the paleontological marvel fascinated him, what mattered more was the light in Anita's eyes.

"That's all there is to see for now." She rose. "Are you hungry?"

"Starved. I never ate lunch."

"Pete's is holding a table for us," she said. "Let's head across the square. I want to hear all about this exciting new commission of yours over dinner."

GORDON POINTED with his fork at the last bite of the strawberry pie he and Anita had shared. "It's all yours."

"It's soooo good," she said, "but I'm about to burst. If you can't handle it, we'll have to break tradition and not clean our plate."

"I'll bet we'd be the first diners to send any of this back." He speared the bite and popped it into his mouth. "Laura's pies are the best I've ever had."

"As widely traveled as you are," Anita replied, "that's quite a compliment. Since you'll be spending most of the summer in France, you'll have the chance to test that claim."

"French patisseries offer tarts rather than pies," Gordon said. "They're thinner and more delicate, but I prefer the

American version. Still, some cafés in Paris make traditional pies for homesick Americans. Why don't you come with me this summer? We'll do a taste test together. I'll wager Laura still wins."

Anita laughed softly. "As if."

"I'm serious." Gordon leaned toward her. "I'm inviting you to Europe with me this summer."

Her smile faltered. "Won't you be busy with your client, going to all those French flea markets … what do you call them?"

"*Marché aux puces*. Or *brocantes*. My client may attend a few, but most of the time I'll be hunting for items on my own. You love treasure-hunting here—I thought you'd adore it over there. You might even find sewing machines for your museum."

Anita rocked back in her chair. "Good heavens, Gordon—you're serious."

"Of course."

Her spine stiffened. "I still have my own business. Archer's Bridal won't run itself. I can't just take off for weeks at a time."

"You're upset," he said gently.

"My shop and the museum are both important to me."

"I understand that. I never said they weren't." He opened his palms. "You told me Louise could handle the bridal shop's daily operations when you opened the museum. And you said you'd hire a bookkeeper if need be. I thought you had plans in place to step away from the day-to-day."

She hesitated. "Fiona did tell me that the excavation could

take months, now that it's possible they'll find a complete skeleton. I won't open the museum until they finish. So, yes ... it is the perfect time." Her defensiveness softened into a smile. "I'm sorry. It's a lovely invitation. Sometimes I can't believe such a kind, successful man is interested in me."

"And sometimes," Gordon said, covering her hands with his, "I can't understand what such a smart, creative woman sees in me. Think of the fun we'd have. I'd love to spend a month in France with you, but even a week in Paris would be magical."

She held his gaze and drew a deep breath.

"You don't have to answer now," he said. "I fly back on Tuesday, and I'll be in France for two months. Join me anytime."

They sat with hands entwined until their server appeared.

"Anything else tonight?"

"Just the check," Gordon said, dropping Anita's hands. Once he paid the bill, they headed out.

"There's Alex and Marc," Anita said, spotting them at another table. "I'd love to say hello—and ask what he thinks about the skull."

"Will he know already?"

"Fiona called Maggie, who was going to put out a press release. Alex would have seen it by now." She crossed the room.

"I'm glad we're not the only ones keeping Pete's open late," Anita said brightly.

"Anita," Alex said, pushing back his chair.

"No need to get up. I just wondered what you thought of the press release."

"Press release?"

"About the rib and the skull they found in the basement."

Alex scrolled through his phone, frowning. "I don't see a release."

"I guess it hasn't gone out yet. Fiona's crew found the skull this afternoon."

"Does that mean they may have the entire skeleton?" Marc asked.

Anita nodded. "Instead of just a tusk, Westbury may have a whole mastodon." She turned to Alex. "What do you think, Mr. Mayor?"

"That's fantastic news! Are you sure you don't want to keep this guy yourself?"

"I already have whiskey bottles and sewing machines. This mastodon deserves its own museum."

"I couldn't agree more," Alex said. "Was it exciting when they uncovered it?"

"I imagine so," Anita replied. "I was at my shop. Fiona showed Sam and me afterward and gave us a short dissertation on life in the Ice Age. Gordon missed it, though—he didn't arrive in town until after she'd left."

Alex tilted his head, studying Gordon. "You weren't driving out of a parking garage late this afternoon?"

The bottom dropped out of Gordon's stomach. He shook his head.

"I only ask because I passed someone leaving as I was driving in. I could've sworn it was you."

Gordon forced a shrug. “Everyone has a double.” He managed a thin smile.

Alex’s gaze lingered. “Then yours is in Westbury.”

CHAPTER 20

"You ready?" Alex asked, glancing at Marc.

"Let me finish my coffee." Marc lifted his cup. "They brewed a pot of decaf for me. I hate to leave a full cup sitting here."

Alex picked up his phone, scrolling once more. "Still nothing." He set it face down on the table.

"Looking for that press release?"

Alex nodded.

"I'm sure the college will put it out tomorrow."

Alex gave him a side-eye.

"What's wrong?" Marc studied him. "You were in a great mood when we came in. Now you look as gloomy as the weather."

The corners of Alex's mouth turned up briefly but fell back into a grim line. "It's not the press release itself. It's what's behind it that bothers me."

Marc raised an eyebrow. "You've lost me. Explain."

"Maggie didn't put out that press release because she doesn't want me to know there's an entire mastodon skeleton down there."

Marc froze, his cup halfway to his lips. "Does this have anything to do with that chat you had with her after the groundbreaking?"

Alex gave a noncommittal shrug.

"The one where you practically sprinted away from her," Marc added.

"You're exaggerating."

"Not by much." Marc leaned back. "We've been together long enough—I can tell when you're dodging. And Maggie? She looked upset. What's really going on?"

Alex rubbed his face with both hands. "I did something that might affect her—and not in a good way. I'm not proud of it."

Marc set down his cup. "That doesn't sound like you. Tell me more."

Alex relayed his conversation with Fiona.

Marc listened, then said, "It's a free country, Alex. You can offer a job to whomever you want."

"I know. And I'll do what's best for Westbury. That's my job. But when Maggie came up to me after the groundbreaking, I got the feeling she already knew I'd spoken to Fiona. At that point, they hadn't found the skull. The museum district idea felt speculative. I figured I'd have time to give Maggie a courtesy call later."

"In a perfect world, you would've looped her in first?"

"Of course. Given our history, that would have been the decent thing to do."

Marc tapped a finger against his cup. "So what stopped you?"

Alex hesitated. "Timing. Circumstances."

"You care about her," Marc said gently. "Which is good. But sometimes caring makes us overprotective. You tried to spare her feelings by keeping quiet, and now you're carrying guilt on top of it."

Alex blew out a breath. "I basically lied to her. And I hate that."

Marc folded his arms. "You ducked her because you didn't want to hurt her—or yourself. Because you knew she'd be upset, and you didn't want to sit in that discomfort."

Alex winced.

Marc leaned in. "You can fix this. Call her and be honest. She may not like it, but at least you'll respect yourself again. And so will she."

Alex nodded slowly. "I need to do it in person. Not over the phone."

"Good. But do it soon. We're seeing Maggie at Susan and Aaron's baby shower. If you don't clear the air before then, it's going to be awkward for everyone."

Alex sagged back in his chair. "You're right. I'd forgotten about that."

Marc rose from the table. "It's late. You don't need the perfect words tonight. Sleep on it. Clarity comes easier in the morning."

Alex gave him a rueful smile. "You always say that."

"That's because it's true." Marc clapped him lightly on the shoulder as they stood. Together they headed out into the night, the neon sign above the bistro going dark behind them.

CHAPTER 21

Grace spotted headlights sweeping across the driveway as she walked from the bedroom wing toward the kitchen. The twins had been asleep for almost an hour, and she'd just finished reading Nicole a bedtime story. Sean was in the family room, absorbed in his video game. Grace had asked if he wanted to hang out, but he'd politely declined.

She opened the front door just as Marissa, still in her grocery store smock embroidered with her name, fumbled in her purse for her key.

"I *thought* that was you coming home," Grace said.

Marissa smiled, stepping inside. They hugged. "The store was slow tonight, so they sent a couple of us home early. My coworker gave me a ride."

"Perfect," Grace said. "Now we'll have time to catch up before your parents get home."

"I was hoping for that, too." Marissa's eyes sparkled. "The littles are asleep?"

Grace nodded. "And Sean's glued to his PlayStation."

"Of course he is," Marissa said with a smirk. "He complains constantly that he only gets one night a week to play."

Grace laughed. "Now I don't feel so bad that he didn't want to hang out with me."

"I'm going to change out of my uniform," Marissa said.

"I'll be in the kitchen, cleaning up the after-dinner mess."

"Be right back—I'll help you."

Grace headed to the kitchen and began loading the dishwasher. Marissa appeared in the doorway, now in jeans and a T-shirt. The two chatted easily about school, Marissa's dance troupe, and her job while tidying the kitchen.

"Why not work at one of your dad's restaurants?" Grace asked.

Marissa rolled her eyes. "I tried. But everyone treated me like a spy because I'm the boss's daughter. It was awful."

"That wouldn't be much fun."

"I lasted a week." Marissa grinned. "This job is better. I started as a bagger, and they have already promoted me to checkout. I've made friends, too."

Grace smiled. "That's great. You know what they say—if you enjoy what you do, you'll never work a day in your life."

"I've never heard that, but it makes sense." Marissa tilted her head. "What about you? Are you still considering a career in journalism? I saw you scribbling notes at the groundbreaking."

Grace started the dishwasher and picked up her water tumbler. "I've changed my mind," she said.

Marissa poured herself a glass of milk. "Tell me everything."

They settled on the living-room sofa. "I love working on the school newspaper, but journalism jobs are scarce," Grace explained. "I want a career that's stable."

Marissa leaned in, listening.

"You remember my brother Tommy's eye surgeries?"

Marissa nodded. "But he's fine now, right?"

"Thank goodness, yes. But his experiences gave me a lot of exposure to the medical field. I've decided to become a physician assistant."

"That's so cool! We see a PA when we go to the doctor. Have you changed your major?"

"Highpointe doesn't offer that program. I'll have to go elsewhere to become a PA. And, to apply, I need both a bachelor's degree and hands-on medical experience. I decided EMT training is the fastest path. I can get certified in six months to a year, work as an EMT, and finish my bachelor's part-time."

Marissa's eyes widened. "You've planned this all out!"

"I have." Grace's voice was steady. "I've been accepted into a top EMT program in the San Francisco area. There are lots of job openings there for after I'm certified, and schools that will accept my Highpointe credits for my bachelor's. It's the perfect plan."

Marissa tucked her feet under her. "You're really moving all the way to California?"

"It's not *that* far." The hesitation in her voice belied her words.

"What do your parents think?"

"My dad wasn't thrilled at first. I go to Highpointe tuition-free because he's a professor there. But he came around. My mom's been supportive from the start. She said I've worked hard, and they'll help me reach my dream. She even offered to get a second job if needed."

"That's amazing."

"They're the best," Grace said warmly. "Just like yours are. Did Frank get upset when you quit the restaurant?"

Marissa shook her head. "He said he understood."

"See?" Grace smiled. "Supportive parents all around."

"When do you start EMT school?"

"The end of August. Mom and I are heading to San Francisco in July to find an apartment for me."

"Wow." Marissa grinned. "Excited?"

"And nervous," Grace admitted. "I've never even lived in a dorm. Now I'll be in my own place. I feel ready—but the thought of not knowing anyone is scary."

"You know David," Marissa said casually. "He lives in San Rafael. That's really close to San Francisco."

Grace's throat tightened. She turned away.

"I saw the two of you at the groundbreaking," Marissa pressed. "You're friends."

"We barely spoke," Grace said softly. "I was hoping he'd come talk to me at the reception afterward, but every time I glanced at him, he looked away."

Marissa popped onto her knees. "Do you still *like* him?" she asked, emphasizing the romantic meaning of the word.

Grace nodded, slow and shy. "I've been thinking about him the whole time he's been away. And when I saw him again … my heart did backflips."

"I thought you had a boyfriend at Highpointe."

"I did. But I ended it. It wasn't the same as with David."

Marissa practically bounced on the sofa. "Grace! This is perfect!"

"What do you mean?"

"I overheard Mom and Frank talking. He and Glenn took David to breakfast before he flew back to California. David told them he realized he still likes you, but was too tongue-tied to talk. He was all down-in-the-dumps, and worried you had a boyfriend. Frank promised him that Mom would find out—and they'd tell David tomorrow."

Grace's breath caught, her hand flying to her chest. "He still likes me?"

Marissa beamed. "Frank said he was miserable. Glenn told him to reach out, but David wanted to be sure you're not with someone else first. Once he knows you're single, he promised to contact you."

Tears filled Grace's eyes. "This is the best news."

"I wish I'd known sooner you'd broken up with your boyfriend!" Marissa said. "I hated thinking David might get hurt all over again."

Grace sprang up and grabbed her purse.

"What're you doing?"

"I can't wait until your parents get home. I've got a better idea." Grace's eyes shone as she pulled out her phone.

Grace's hands trembled as she unlocked her phone and scrolled to David's number in her contacts.

Marissa watched her, eyes wide. "What are you going to say?" Marissa whispered.

"I don't know," Grace admitted. She hovered over her phone, her heart racing like it was trying to break free from her chest. "If I overthink it, I'll never do it." Her thumbs flew across the screen.

Hi David. It was good … She pressed the delete key repeatedly. *It was so great to see you at the groundbreaking. I wish we could have talked.*

Her finger froze over the send button.

Marissa leaned closer. "That's perfect. Simple. Friendly. Not too much."

Grace exhaled and hit send. For a moment, the room felt suspended in silence.

Both girls watched the screen. Seconds later, three little undulating dots appeared.

"He's typing!" Marissa squealed, hugging a pillow to her chest.

Grace's pulse pounded in her ears. She forced herself to breathe.

David's reply came:

I've been kicking myself for not going up to you. I wanted to. I just didn't know what to say. Can I call?

Grace's knees went weak. She sank onto the sofa beside Marissa and showed her the screen.

"I told you!" Marissa was gleeful. "He *likes* you!"

Grace's thumbs shook as she typed back:

Yes. Tomorrow? I'm babysitting tonight.

Whenever works for you. I've wanted to talk to you for a long time.

Grace closed her eyes, tears slipping down her cheeks. Across from her, Marissa silently pumped her fist in the air.

CHAPTER 22

Grace thought about nothing but David on the drive home from Frank and Loretta's. They had been genuinely delighted that she and David were going to talk the next day. Today, actually, she reminded herself. It was after midnight. She didn't know how she'd ever get to sleep—she was anxious to hear his voice.

She pulled into her driveway and let herself into the quiet house. Her parents and Tommy were asleep. Magellan, their cat, lifted her head a fraction of an inch in greeting as Grace walked past her, perched on the back of the sofa.

Grace had become a typical college-student night owl, and usually relished the peacefulness of the house after everyone else had gone to bed. Tonight, however, it felt lonely. She went to her room and flopped back on her bed. She held her phone above her face and reread her text exchange with David. Acting on impulse, she texted: *I'm home now, if you're still up.*

Her phone buzzed almost immediately. Grace pressed "accept," her breath catching when she heard his voice.

"Grace?"

"Yes," she whispered.

"Grace?" David's voice was low, almost hesitant, as if he wasn't sure she'd really answered.

"Yes. It's me."

For a moment, neither spoke. The silence felt charged—like the air right before a summer storm.

"I've been wanting to talk to you since I saw you. Actually … longer than that."

"I wanted to talk to *you,* too. But every time I looked over, you …" She trailed off, suddenly shy.

"I chickened out," he admitted with a sardonic laugh. "I saw you standing there, looking so confident and beautiful, and the words I wanted to say got stuck in my throat."

"My insides felt like a cement mixer. I was anything but confident."

Both of them laughed then—soft, almost disbelieving.

"I've thought about you every day since I've been in California. I realized right away that I didn't want to break up. But then I heard you were dating someone …"

"I broke it off with him because it … it wasn't you." Grace's hand tightened on the phone. Her eyes stung. "I've been thinking about you, too. More than I wanted to admit."

David let out a breath, and she could almost hear the

weight lifting from him. "Do you know how much it means to hear you say that?"

Grace rolled onto her side. "So … what do we do now?"

"I'm in California for the foreseeable future. But I don't want distance to get in our way this time. We can text, call, video chat. And I'd love for you to come out and visit."

Her heart did a somersault. "I'm actually moving to the San Francisco area in August for school. EMT training. Then on to PA school, hopefully."

He nearly choked. "Wait—you're serious? You're moving here?"

"Yes." Grace smiled through her tears. "Very soon."

The stunned joy in his voice wrapped around her like a warm blanket. "Then maybe … this is our second chance."

Grace hugged her pillow. "I think it is."

They chatted for two hours about school, family, favorite movies they hadn't seen together, and all the little things they'd missed in each other's lives. Every shared memory brought them closer together, until the rip in their relationship was repaired.

At last, Grace's voice grew heavy with sleep. "David?"

"Mm?"

"I'm really glad we didn't let us slip away."

When she hung up, the silence of the house no longer felt empty. It felt full of promise.

CHAPTER 23

Gordon glanced at Anita. She sat at one end of her kitchen table, hunched over her laptop. He was doing the same at the opposite end.

She looked up at him as if sensing his gaze. "Look at the two of us," she said. "It's a perfect summer Sunday, and we've spent the entire day inside working away on our laptops instead of being outside enjoying nature."

"Your windows and back door are open," he pointed out with a smile. "There's a pleasant breeze in here. That counts as enjoying nature. Besides, we're both happy with what we're doing. I can tell by the pages of notes you've scribbled on that legal pad that you're uncovering a lot of good information."

She put down her pen and stretched her arms over her head, leaning back in her chair. "I've found several ideas for niche museums," she said.

"I thought you might be researching ideas for this new museum district. What have you come up with?"

She picked up her pad and flipped to the first page. "Ideas that are in keeping with my sewing machine museum are museums devoted to bobbins, thread, sewing patterns, quilting, or yarn. Robert Harris is a rare book dealer, so I thought he might have contacts interested in starting a printing press museum. Or one devoted to the book as art—paintings and sculptures of books, art-themed décor—that sort of thing."

"Those are interesting ideas," Gordon said. "A small appliance museum would be a good fit with your sewing machines, but there's already one nearby."

A smile brightened her features like a fresh coat of paint. "I remember, Gordon. You took me there to show me what my museum could look like."

"The owner was happy with its location next to his hardware store," Gordon replied. "But if he ever wanted to expand, I think he'd do well in a municipal museum district. Anything else?"

"I've read about museums dedicated to dolls, puppets, miniatures, and theater props and memorabilia. Basically, if people are interested in collecting something, you can start a museum focused on it."

"What do you plan to do with this information?" Gordon asked.

Anita shrugged. "I don't know. I guess I was just interested. Once I got going after lunch, I couldn't stop."

"I've got an idea for you," Gordon said.

She raised one eyebrow. "I'm all ears."

"Put that information into a report."

Anita groaned. "I'm not in school anymore, Gordon."

He chuckled. "I don't mean like a book report, but at least document the ideas you've come up with."

"Why would I need to do that?"

"You said Alex is going to present the idea of a museum district to the town council. Will they take comments from the public?"

Anita pursed her lips. "At the very least. When they make big changes in Westbury, they hold public hearings. People love living here because our elected officials listen to input from residents."

"There you go," Gordon said. "Write up your notes now, and you'll be ready to speak when the time comes."

"I've never spoken at a public hearing in my life, Gordon. I don't intend to start now."

"Anita." His tone was serious. "Remember how nervous you were before your remarks at the grand opening of your sewing machine exhibit at the Highpointe College Library?"

"I do. That's why I don't want to speak again."

"Have you forgotten that your speech hit it out of the park?" he asked. "You were nervous when you started, but you held the attention of every person in the audience. You're a terrific public speaker, sweetheart. You have nothing to be afraid of."

She bit the corner of her mouth, but her eyes began to dance. "You really think anyone will be interested in my ideas for a museum district?"

"I'm positive," Gordon said.

She rose from her chair. "It's almost four. I'd better see what I have on hand for supper."

"Don't worry about cooking," Gordon said. "I'll run to Pete's and bring back takeout. Type up your notes while they're fresh in your mind."

"I appreciate that. This is going to be a busy week at the shop because my workroom supervisor is visiting her mother in Arizona. If I don't do it now, I won't get back to it for another week." She moved along the table toward him. "What are you working on?"

Gordon slammed his laptop shut. A dozen tabs were open, all of them dealing with restoring a historic home. He'd researched the history of his new property in the public records, investigated the requirements for obtaining historic designation, and studied the best methods for returning a mansion to its former glory. He wasn't ready, however, to bring Anita into the picture.

She gave him a quizzical look.

"I'm starved," he said, deflecting her attention. "Do you mind if we eat early?"

"No," she said. "By the time we place the order and you pick it up, it'll be dinnertime anyway."

"Do you know what you'd like?"

"The Sunday special is fine by me."

He scrolled through his phone to the menu. "That's roast chicken in a tarragon pan jus, Yukon Gold mashed potatoes, and roasted carrots?"

"That's the one."

"I'll make it two," he replied. "Dessert?"

"Surprise me."

He got up from the table. "Finish your report. I'm done for the day." He slipped his laptop into his satchel and zipped it shut. The gesture was casual, but the quickness of it carried a quiet weight—a secret tucked safely away for now.

"It's going to be a beautiful evening," he added. "Want to go for a walk after supper?"

"You read my mind. Can we stroll by the houses around the square? It's a two-and-a-half-mile round-trip, but it's my favorite walk."

"Sounds good to me."

He placed their dinner order and headed for his car as Anita bent once more over her laptop, fingers flying across the keys.

GORDON CIRCLED the square twice on the busy Sunday, searching for a parking spot. At last, he spotted a car pulling away from the curb four doors down from Celebrations and slid his rental into the space.

The late-afternoon sun had begun its slow descent toward the western horizon. He ambled along the sidewalk, admiring the canopy of green from the trees on the square against the azure blue of the cloudless sky. Children ran and shouted to each other, couples strolled hand-in-hand, and people walked dogs of every size and description. His heart swelled with contentment. Westbury would be a wonderful place to call home.

"Gordon!"

The voice broke into his reverie. He turned to see Susan coming out of Celebrations.

"Hello, Susan," he said. "You're looking well. I heard the wedding might've been a bit too much for you." He faltered, suddenly aware that commenting on a pregnant woman's health felt like murky territory.

"That was nothing. Mainly, it was an overzealous concern by my surgeon husband. I'm fine." She pulled him in for a hug. "I'm glad I ran into you. I saw you at my office building on Wednesday. You stepped off the elevator and practically sprinted across the lobby. You would've thought the place was on fire. I called to you, but you must not have heard me."

Gordon's stomach plummeted like an elevator with a severed cable. "You must've been mistaken," he said carefully. "That wasn't me."

"Oh?" Susan stepped back, her expression full of disbelief.

"I'm afraid I must have a doppelgänger," he said. "Alex mentioned he thought he saw me coming out of the parking garage that same afternoon. Must've been the same man."

"Good heavens," Susan said. "You really do have a twin out there. How odd! I've never seen him before, and Westbury isn't that big."

"Maybe he doesn't live around here, or he was just here on business or something," Gordon offered, doubling down on the lie. He cleared his throat. "I'd better let you go. I'm on my way to Pete's to pick up dinner for Anita and me."

"I'd better be on my way, too," Susan said. "I've been registering at Celebrations for my upcoming baby shower, and I thought I'd be home an hour ago. Have a nice dinner. Give Anita my love."

"Will do," Gordon replied. He turned and continued walking toward Pete's, his thoughts in turmoil. How many people had seen him on Wednesday afternoon? One thing was certain: in Westbury, you couldn't get away with anything.

CHAPTER 24

Alistair

The aroma of coffee roused me from my slumber. I drifted down from my attic and intercepted John as he climbed the stairs, a steaming mug in his hand. Naturally, I spun around and followed close behind.

Maggie was in bed, propped against her pillows, with her knees bent and her laptop balanced in front of her.

"I thought you were getting a late start," John said, setting the coffee on her nightstand.

"I've decided to work from home this morning." Maggie pushed her glasses up her nose. "I want to complete my commencement address before I head into the office."

"I thought you finished that yesterday."

"That's what I told you," she admitted, her tone edged with frustration. "But I'm not satisfied. I've been rereading it this morning, and ... it needs work."

I couldn't help but agree. I'd hovered over her shoulder the afternoon before when she'd closed the laptop and declared herself finished. The speech had been flat—uninspired, dreary even. That wasn't like my Maggie. Her words usually soared, full of courage and hope. Yesterday's draft was a snooze fest, as they say these days. I suspected it reflected the cloud hanging over her after her conversation with Alex following the groundbreaking.

"Do you want me to look at it?" John asked, leaning over.

"No." She snapped the laptop shut. "I know it's bad. I'll fix it this morning. You can read it later." She looked up at him. "Thanks for the coffee," she said, her tone softening. "I know you need to get going."

He disappeared into the bathroom and picked up his toothbrush. "What else is on your agenda today?"

"The press release about the mastodon skull goes out this morning. I already approved the final draft. Josh and Colleen will post it."

"Will you call Alex to make sure he sees it?"

Her voice chilled. "No. He will."

"Maybe if you gave him a heads-up, he'd tell you about his plans for the museum district—"

"And about offering Fiona a job with the city?" Her laugh was sharp. "I already gave him that chance at the groundbreaking. He covered it up. If he wants to tell me his plans, the ball's in his court."

Her feet hit the floor with a thump.

John raised his hands in surrender. "Okay, sweetheart. I

don't want to get into this again. Do whatever you think is best."

"Thank you." Her tone was icy enough to frost the mirror.

He kissed her cheek. "I've got to go. See you tonight. I look forward to reading your revised speech."

She took her coffee into the bathroom, shower cap already at the ready. I knew I had thirty minutes before she came downstairs. Thirty minutes to help her find her spark again.

I glided to the library. Roman and Eve were curled in their baskets, tails twitching in their sleep, while Buttercup sprawled along the sofa's back, radiating disdain.

The shelves beckoned. Maggie and John had filled a few with their own favorites, but most of the volumes were older, the kind I loved—leather spines, gilt lettering, dust that whispered of decades undisturbed.

She needed inspiration. I wanted her to rediscover her voice of courage and resilience. I scanned until I found the books I was looking for: Bartlett's *Familiar Quotations* and Tryon Edwards' *A Dictionary of Thoughts*. Perfect. My excitement made me tremble.

But how to make her notice? From the desk chair, I tested the view—pulling each book forward by an inch. Too subtle. Unless she was searching for them, she'd never see the books. I bore down, channeling every ounce of my telepathic energy. One book slipped, then the other, tumbling to the floor beside the chair with a satisfying thud.

Both lay open, spines flat. Bartlett's revealed Henry David

Thoreau: "Go confidently in the direction of your dreams. Live the life you have imagined." Edwards' dictionary offered Ralph Waldo Emerson: "What lies behind us and what lies before us are tiny matters compared to what lies within us."

I somersaulted midair in triumph. If these weren't perfect, I didn't know what was. And even if she didn't use these, she'd surely be drawn into their pages, searching for more.

Her footsteps sounded on the stairs. I zipped back to the sofa, nestling beside Buttercup, who ignored me, as usual. From this perch, I'd have a perfect view of her laptop screen.

She would rewrite that speech. And her words would be remembered for the rest of those graduates' lives. I could hardly wait.

CHAPTER 25

Gordon retrieved Anita's satchel from the cubby by her garage door and carried it to the car for her.

"Thank you for letting me work at your place today," he said.

"Of course." She gave him an apologetic grin. "I haven't been to the grocery in ages, so I'm not sure what you'll find in my fridge for lunch."

"Don't worry about me," Gordon said. "I'm so busy, I'll work through lunch anyway."

They exchanged a quick kiss, and Anita was on her way to work.

Gordon returned to the kitchen and settled in at the table, drilling down on his research into renovating the old mansion he'd just purchased. The quiet of Anita's house wrapped around him, steadying his focus.

His phone rang just before eleven.

"Morning, Tim," Gordon said.

"I arranged a meeting at the house with Sam and Jeff," Tim said. "I know you're leaving town tomorrow and won't be back in Westbury until late this summer. Care to join us?"

"Today?" Gordon asked, a smile playing at his lips.

"Right now," Tim said. "They're on their way over to the house."

Gordon was already out of his chair. "I thought they were too busy with the museum renovations to meet."

"They've completed everything except for the final touches needed right before the museum opens. The mastodon skeleton has delayed the opening indefinitely, so they have time to fill. Sam and Jeff can start work on the house immediately."

"Whoa." Gordon shut his laptop and shoved it into his satchel. "I'm on my way."

He locked Anita's house and headed for his car parked at the curb. The prospect of beginning renovations sooner than expected thrilled him. It also meant he needed to speed up his plan to get Anita to Paris.

Gordon made the short drive to the house with his mind spinning. Visions of restored woodwork and gleaming chandeliers tumbled together with images of Anita's hand in his, strolling along the Seine. His emotions ranged from elated to frightened.

He pulled to the curb behind Sam's truck and sat for a moment, steadying himself. Organization. Control. Facts. That was his comfort zone. He needed to be there again before stepping inside to meet with the men who were rapidly becoming close friends.

ANITA TURNED onto her street and drove the short distance to her house. Gordon's car wasn't parked at the curb. She pulled into her driveway and picked up the bag from the sandwich shop.

Earlier that morning, she'd placed an online order for her usual turkey and provolone on whole wheat. When she arrived at the shop to pick it up, she'd added an Italian sub for Gordon. She figured he'd love the delicious sandwich and could eat it as he worked. He shouldn't skip lunch.

She hurried through her front door and headed to the kitchen. His computer and satchel were gone. She scanned the room for a note from him but didn't find one. "That's not surprising," she told herself. "He didn't know I was going to bring him a sandwich. He thought I would be at the bridal shop the entire day."

Anita put Gordon's sub in the refrigerator and set the bag of chips on the kitchen table. She tore a piece of paper from her grocery list pad and scribbled a note:

Your favorite sub is in the fridge—figured you'd be hungry. Hope you like it! xoxo, A

She propped the note beside the chips and retraced her steps to the car.

For a moment, she considered texting him—but decided it would be fun to let him discover the surprise on his own when he returned to her place. She was parking in her spot behind the bridal shop when it occurred to her: maybe Gordon had gone out to buy lunch. She gathered her purse and sandwich and headed inside, newly resolved to text him after all.

One of her seamstresses called out as soon as she stepped through the back door.

"Anita—we've got a big problem. The lace we received from Italy this morning is defective. Only a tiny part of it is usable."

Anita abandoned her purse and sandwich on the break room counter and hurried to the workroom, her employee's worried tone overriding any thoughts of texting Gordon.

~

THE MEN WERE STANDING in the overgrown yard when Gordon walked up. Sam raised a hand in greeting, while Jeff was bent over, studying the porch steps.

"Morning," Gordon said, shaking each man's hand.

"Thanks for calling us," Sam replied. "We took a quick walk around. She's got good bones, Gordon. Needs work—I'm sure nothing is up to code—but the house is solid."

Jeff tapped one boot against a sagging step. "These'll have to be replaced. Safety first."

"I expected as much," Gordon said. He tried to keep his voice even, but his pulse thrummed with anticipation. His gaze traveled to the top of the three-story façade. Would this be where, one day, he would live his life as a married man?

Tim clapped him on the shoulder. "Let's head inside." He unlocked the heavy front door, its brass knob tarnished with age. The hinges groaned in protest as he pushed it open. A draft of cool, stale air met them, tinged with dust and something faintly sweet—maybe remnants of woodsmoke from a long-ago fire in one of the massive hearths.

The men stepped into the foyer. Sunlight filtered through tall windows, catching motes of dust that danced in the air.

"Look at that staircase," Sam murmured. He ran a hand along the carved newel post, its surface nicked and worn but still majestic. The sweeping staircase curved gracefully toward the second floor, its banister lined with intricate scrollwork.

Jeff whistled low. "You don't see craftsmanship like this anymore."

They moved from room to room, assessing. Sam took notes in a small leather-bound notebook. Jeff ran his fingers along cracked plaster walls, pressed at floorboards, and muttered measurements under his breath.

"This dining room will seat twelve comfortably," Tim said. "Once the plaster's repaired and the floors refinished, it'll be magnificent."

"And the pocket doors," Sam added, sliding one halfway open. "They'll be smooth as butter after a little work." He addressed Gordon. "You'll want to prioritize roof repairs and electrical first. Once the house is watertight and safe, the rest can follow."

Gordon nodded.

They ended the first-floor tour in the grand parlor, its

high ceiling adorned with an elegant medallion. Gordon turned in a slow circle, taking in the faded grandeur of his new house. He took a deep breath and turned to Sam and Jeff. "I assume the kitchen and bathrooms are complete tearouts."

"The kitchen is, for sure," Jeff agreed. "My guess is the bathrooms will be as well. Let's take a look."

Gordon held up a hand. "Before we go any farther, are you interested in restoring this place for me?"

"Definitely!" Sam said, looking at Jeff, who nodded his agreement.

"This will be as interesting as restoring the Olsson House," Jeff said. "I wish we could capture the process on film," he said. "It'll be extremely interesting."

"Like *This Old House,*" Sam chuckled. "Only on steroids."

"That's a great idea!" Gordon's eyes widened with a sudden thought. "Did you meet Maggie and John's friends from New England? The ones who host a show like that?"

"Pam Olson and Steve Turner," Jeff said. "Charming couple."

"What's the name of their show?" Gordon narrowed his eyes and rubbed his forehead.

"*Wishes of Home,*" Jeff supplied. "We joked about doing a joint project together when they were here last Thanksgiving."

"Well …" Gordon's voice radiated excitement. "It's not a joke now. Would you want a joint project—if they're available? You'd be in charge. I'm not taking work away from you."

"Our expertise is in construction and restoration," Sam said. "Melding period design with a modern aesthetic is not. That's Pam's area."

"I agree," Jeff said. "If we can enlist their help, I'm all for it."

"Let's get on with our tour," Gordon said. "Will one of you contact them for me?"

Sam and Jeff looked to Tim.

"I'd be happy to," Tim said. "Who knows? Westbury could become a lucrative source of business for them."

With a renewed sense of purpose, the four men headed to the upper floors.

CHAPTER 26

"I'll put together a detailed work plan and cost estimate for the structural renovations by the end of next week," Jeff said as the men returned to the first floor.

"That'd be great," Gordon replied. "I'm eager to get started on the new roof and structural repairs as soon as possible. I'll be in Europe the entire summer—will that pose a problem?"

"It shouldn't," Sam said. He jerked his thumb toward Jeff. "This one's technologically proficient. He'll send you videos, and we can always communicate by … what's that called?" He looked at his partner.

"FaceTime," Jeff supplied.

Gordon shook hands with each of them. "Remember, other than contacting Pam and Steve, please keep this quiet so Anita doesn't find out I own the place." The others nodded their agreement, and all four men stepped across the threshold onto the front porch. Sam and Jeff headed toward the walkway.

"This'll be the first thing I fix," Jeff said over his shoulder, pointing at the loose step.

Gordon gave him a thumbs-up, then turned to Tim. "It's getting late. I can't believe we were here the entire afternoon. Thanks for spending so much time with us."

"My pleasure," Tim said. "I've been interested in this house since I was a kid. These old mansions around the square are one reason I went into real estate. Want to go back inside?"

Gordon shook his head. "I need to beat feet back to Anita's. She believes I was going to be chained to my computer all day. I'd prefer she didn't find out I was gone most of it."

Tim bit his lip and raised an eyebrow, his expression hovering between curiosity and restraint.

Gordon looked away, not wanting to explain. "I'll tell you about it later, when we have more time."

Tim locked the front door and held out the key.

"That's the only copy, isn't it?" Gordon asked.

Tim nodded.

"Would you mind hanging onto it?" Gordon asked. "Since I'll be in Europe, someone in Westbury needs to have a key. I'd run over to Westbury Hardware to have a copy made, but Anita should be home any minute now."

"I'll hang onto it—no worries," Tim said. "I'm also happy to make copies of it."

"I hate to impose," Gordon replied.

"I'm offering as a friend," Tim said firmly, watching him a beat longer than necessary.

"If you really don't mind, can you make one for me, and a couple of extras—one each for Sam and Jeff?"

"Sure," Tim replied. "I'm happy to help with anything you need while you're away this summer."

"That could turn into quite a bit of work," Gordon said. "I want to pay you for your time."

"Let's wait and see what develops," Tim said.

"All right," Gordon agreed reluctantly, "but I insist on reimbursing you for your expenses."

They walked together along the pathway toward the low iron gate in the fence along the sidewalk.

"All right," Tim said. "I'll keep receipts for anything I spend."

"Beginning with those keys," Gordon replied.

Tim nodded. "I'll let you know the minute I hear back from Pam and Steve," Tim said. "Have a good summer abroad, and don't worry about anything here. You're in good hands with Sam and Jeff."

"I know I am," Gordon said. He met Tim's gaze for a moment, then looked away. "I appreciate your help—and your discretion, Tim."

This part of his plan was coming along well, Gordon thought. It was now time to focus on Anita.

Gordon breathed a sigh of relief when he saw that the space at the curb in front of Anita's house—the one he had vacated earlier—was still open. He pulled his rental car into position and bounded up the steps to the front door.

On a normal weekday, Anita would already be home, he thought. With any luck, he'd replace his laptop and papers on the kitchen table, and she'd find him there when she got home.

He hurried through the living room to the kitchen, pulling his laptop from his satchel as he walked. He set it on the table beside the bag of chips and the note she had left for him. Gordon read the note with mixed emotions. It had been incredibly sweet of her to bring lunch to him. It was just like Anita to be so thoughtful. The gesture warmed his heart. On the other hand, she now knew he hadn't been home the entire day.

What excuse would he give her? His mind whirled. One thing was certain, he couldn't tell her about spending the afternoon at his new house with Tim, Sam, and Jeff. He stood in the kitchen, brows furrowed. After the debacle of both Alex and Susan spotting him leaving his lawyer's office earlier, he knew he needed a solid alibi.

His stomach growled. He tore open the bag of chips and grabbed a handful. The salty crunch awakened rather than satisfied his hunger. He opened the refrigerator and removed the sandwich.

He devoured one bite, then another. She was right—it was delicious.

Gordon leaned against the counter as he chewed, and an

idea flashed into his mind. He would tell Anita that he'd driven by the future home of Forever Guides. He grabbed another handful of chips. Yes, that made sense. He had missed the groundbreaking and wanted to see the site.

He and Frank had exchanged emails that morning. Construction wouldn't begin for another week. That meant that there was nothing to see—and nothing for him to lie about. No one would have noticed if he had driven past the vacant lot. He would thank Anita profusely for the sandwich and tell her he had enjoyed every bite. A satisfied smile spread across his lips. His story was airtight.

Motion outside the kitchen window caught his attention. The garage door was rising. Anita was home. She would walk into the kitchen any second. In a rush, he swept the remains of the chips and the half-eaten sandwich into the trash can, burying them deep in the plastic liner. Swiping the crumbs from his lips, he turned as Anita came through the garage door.

"Hello, darling," he said, crossing to greet her. He took the Tomascino's pizza box from her hands.

"I hope this is okay for dinner," she said. "I texted to see what you wanted, but you didn't answer."

He spun away, setting the box on the counter. His mind raced.

"I put my phone on silent so I could concentrate," he said quickly. "I forgot to take it off silent until just now. You know I love pizza—any kind of pizza. This is perfect." He hoped his smile looked convincing. "Busy day?" he asked, shifting the subject.

"Very," she said, shaking her head. "A few unexpected disasters, but everything turned out fine in the end. I have the most creative and talented staff in the business."

"I can't wait to hear all about it," Gordon said.

She placed her satchel and purse by the door, then brought plates and napkins to the table before sitting down.

"What would you like to drink?" he asked.

"There's diet cola in the fridge," she said. "I always keep that on hand. I know wine's popular with pizza, but, for me? It has to be soda."

He pulled two cans from the refrigerator and set them on the table.

"Did you like your lunch?" she asked, giving him a small, searching look.

"It was absolutely delicious," he replied smoothly. "I ate every bit of it when I got home."

She smiled, but her eyes lingered on him for a moment longer than usual, as if weighing his words. Something didn't quite add up, though she couldn't put her finger on it.

Gordon launched into his story about driving by the Forever Guides site, his voice even and assured. A tiny frisson of guilt slid down his spine. He was lying to the woman he loved—again. *It's all for a good cause,* he told himself. *She'll never find out. There's no harm in this.*

CHAPTER 27

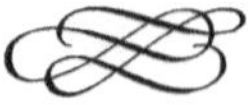

"Mr. Mayor," Tim called to the familiar figure searching through the bins of screws in the aisle ahead of him.

Alex shifted his eyes from the scrap of paper with his shopping list and looked up at Tim. "Good morning, Council Member," Alex said. He shifted the list into his left hand and extended his right to Tim.

The men shook hands.

"What are you doing at Westbury Hardware?" Tim asked.

"Marc and I are giving Aaron and Susan one of those newfangled double strollers for their baby shower gift. The box said 'some' assembly required." He rolled his eyes. "That's the understatement of the century. We spent last weekend working on it, but realized we didn't have all the hardware we needed. Our plan is to finish it this weekend. Since Town Hall is around the corner, I offered to pick up the missing parts. It's such a beautiful morning, I walked over here. I needed to get out of my office and stretch my legs—to think."

"Anything going on at Town Hall I should know about?"

"Did you read the press release about the additional mastodon bones found in Anita's basement?"

Tim nodded.

"I bet you knew about it before the press release went out. You represented Anita in the purchase of that building. I suspect you heard the news right away."

Tim shrugged noncommittally.

"And I'm sure Sam and Jeff knew too, since they're doing the renovations for her."

"There's no such thing as a secret in Westbury," Tim said. "You know that."

"If that's the truth," Alex replied, raising his eyebrows, "you probably already know I've been thinking about revitalizing the downtown by establishing a museum district."

Tim nodded. "It's a great idea."

"If I can convince Anita to donate the mastodon skeleton to the town instead of the college, we'll have a showcase item to launch the whole district—a real wow factor."

"I agree with that too," Tim said.

"I feel like I'm going behind Maggie's back suggesting this," Alex admitted. "But I can't put our friendship and my feelings for her above the town's best interest. That's why I haven't said much until now. Why kick a hornet's nest if I don't have to?"

Tim didn't respond to the rhetorical question.

"But now we've got the prospect of the entire skeleton," Alex continued, "and it's time for me to move forward. Tonya Holmes was in her council office this morning, so I floated the idea by her."

"What did she think?"

"She isn't keen on it." Alex frowned. "Honestly, I was taken aback. We've always been aligned on issues."

"That surprises me, too," Tim said. "Why doesn't she like the idea?"

"She thinks it'll be expensive and take focus away from other things the town needs to address."

"Such as?"

"The usual—public safety, teacher pay, road repair, and maintenance."

"You're not talking about abandoning any of those, are you?"

"Of course not. The district would be in addition to those. We'd need voters to approve an additional sales tax to fund it."

"We could include a bump in funding for those issues, along with the museum district, in that tax increase," Tim suggested. "That might make her feel better."

"Good idea," Alex replied. "I hadn't thought of that."

"What's your next step?"

"I'm preparing a proposal for the town council. I'll suggest a public hearing to consider the district."

"I'll bet Tonya changes her mind," Tim said. "I'm a big supporter of this idea. Let me talk to her. I'll work on getting other council members on board, too."

"Thanks, Tim. Getting it approved will be challenging, but I think it'll be crucial for the growth and success of Westbury."

"What will you do about Maggie?"

"Marc says I need to talk to her—and the sooner the better."

"I agree with him."

"The baby shower's two weeks from Sunday," Alex said. "Marc thinks I should talk to her before then, but, if it doesn't go well, it could make things awkward. I plan to ask her to meet me for coffee on the Monday morning after the shower."

"And your proposal to the council?"

"It'll be in your inbox that Monday morning—right after I talk to Maggie."

"You've thought this through," Tim said.

"I have," Alex replied. "Now—I'd better find the rest of the stuff on this list and get back to Town Hall."

"I need to be going myself," Tim said. "I'm making keys for …" He caught himself before mentioning Gordon's new house. "For one of my listings."

"You're the busiest realtor in town," Alex said with a laugh. "I don't know how you manage both your business and being on the council."

"Look who's talking—mayor, attorney, and stroller-assembly expert."

"The jury's still out on that last one," Alex said.

They shook hands and went their separate ways.

CHAPTER 28

Judy stepped back and assessed the mound of chopped onion on the cutting board in front of her. "That was a small onion," she muttered to herself. "I need more." She grabbed another onion from the wire basket on the counter and quickly reduced it to a neatly diced pile of chopped onion that would have made Julia Child proud.

Jeff entered the kitchen and made a beeline for the coffeepot. "Are we having an army over for dinner that I don't know about?" he teased, refilling his mug.

"I'm making a big batch of turkey chili," Judy said. She glanced into the cast-iron Dutch oven on the stove. "I doubled the recipe so I could take dinner to Sunday and Josh as a welcome-to-the-neighborhood gift."

"That's awfully nice," Jeff replied. "They've been moving in for the last two weeks. Are they finally done?"

Judy nodded. "I ran into Josh walking their dogs this morning. He said they moved in their remaining things yesterday. Last night was their first night to sleep in my"—she caught herself and smiled—"in their house. They're working like crazy to get everything set up. I figured they deserved a home-cooked meal. There's a green salad to go with it, and I'm baking cornbread. I even made chocolate chip cookies."

"You gave it your all. I like it when new people move into our neighborhood." Jeff's eyes drifted across the counter.

"Are you by any chance looking for these cookies?" she asked.

"Well, yeah," he admitted with a grin. "I could smell them from my office upstairs."

She handed him a plastic container, popping off the lid. "Help yourself. I saved some for us."

Jeff picked up a cookie, dunked it into his coffee, and took a bite.

"What are you working on this afternoon?" Judy asked.

"I'm finishing the proposal for Gordon's new house. Sam's coming by later to go over it, and then we'll send it to him."

"I'm thrilled that old beauty is going to be restored to its former glory," Judy said, glancing up at the ceiling. "If it turns out anywhere near as good as this house, it'll be magnificent."

"Thanks, sweetheart," Jeff said warmly. "Sam and I are excited about the project."

Judy heated olive oil in the Dutch oven and slid the

onions into the pot. They sizzled and popped as the kitchen filled with their aroma. She turned to the bowls of green pepper, ground turkey, and spices lined up beside the stove. "You're right," she said. "I've got enough here to feed an army. Let's invite Sam and Joan to join us for dinner. Joan can ride over with Sam and come with me when I take supper to Sunday and Josh."

"That's a great idea." Jeff leaned in to kiss her cheek. "I'll call Sam."

He grabbed a paper napkin from the dispenser and stacked several cookies on top of it. "These will help me power through the rest of the proposal. And remember"—he wagged a finger at her —"Gordon's purchase of that house and the fact that he's restoring it is a secret, at least for now."

Judy rolled her eyes.

"You and Joan are the only ones who know, other than Tim, Sam, and me. You cannot let word slip out."

"I understand," she said. "I can keep a secret with the best of them."

Jeff tilted his head and raised an eyebrow.

"What?" she asked indignantly. "Are you saying I have loose lips?"

He didn't answer.

"I'm taking those back," Judy declared, lunging for his cookies.

Jeff clutched them to his chest and bolted out of the kitchen.

"It's a good thing you're fast!" Judy called after him. She turned back to the stove, stirring the caramelizing onions.

With a sly smile, she reached for her own chocolate chip cookie.

"You're sure they're home?" Joan asked.

"I texted Sunday earlier this afternoon, and she said they'd be there the rest of the day. I told her we'd drop off their supper." Judy ladled a final scoop of turkey chili into an insulated bowl and covered it with foil. She seized the handles with potholders. "I'm sure glad you're here, Joan. I couldn't manage all of this on my own."

"I'll carry the salad, cornbread, and cookies," Joan replied.

They poked their heads into the library on their way to the front door.

"We're headed over to Sunday and Josh's," Judy said, lifting the bowl with both hands. "Will you be ready to eat when we get back?"

Jeff and Sam looked at each other and nodded. "We're done," Jeff said. "We'll send the proposal to Gordon now."

"Remember, ladies," Sam said, "mum's the word about our project."

"We know," the women said indignantly, and headed out the door.

"I can't wait to see what the kids have done with the place," Judy said as they walked.

"Me too," Joan replied. "New owners always make changes to a place, so it feels like their own. Are you sure you won't," she paused, glancing at her friend, "get your feelings hurt? You were always so proprietary about that house."

"No way," Judy replied. "I'll be fine. As a matter of fact, when I moved into the Olsson house, I realized how badly my place needed updating."

Joan nodded with a tiny shrug, acknowledging she'd heard her friend but didn't fully believe her.

They walked up the front steps, their presence announced by the vociferous barking of Dan and Cara before they even rang the doorbell.

"Down, you two," Josh called as he opened the door. The dogs danced excitedly at his legs, tails wagging furiously, before settling into reluctant sits at his command.

Joan and Judy stepped inside.

"That smells amazing," Josh said. "Here, let me help." He reached for the bowl.

"It's hot," Judy warned. "I'll carry it to the kitchen."

"You know the way," Josh said with a smile. Dan and Cara broke their stay just long enough to trot after the women before circling back to Josh, clearly hoping for praise.

Judy and Joan wove their way to the kitchen through boxes stacked in the hallway. Sunday stood at the sink, drying crystal glasses and placing them on the top shelf of a cupboard.

"That's where I used to keep my good crystal," Judy said.

"I love knowing that," Sunday replied. "It means I picked the right place to store them."

The women set their food on the counter.

"Organizing a kitchen is a huge job," Joan said. "I carefully considered how I'd use the space, but, in the end, I always rearranged a few cupboards or drawers to better suit me."

Sunday placed the glass she had been drying into the cupboard, tossed her dish towel over her shoulder, and hugged each of the older women.

"I believe it's your nature to plan things out carefully," Joan said. "Just don't be too hard on yourself if you need to make adjustments."

Josh stepped around the women and slipped his arm around Sunday's shoulders. "You've nailed her to a T, ladies." He kissed the top of his wife's head. "That's sound advice."

"It's so nice of you to bring us dinner," Sunday said. "And very much appreciated. We've eaten pizza more often in the last month than I did when I was in college. Suffice it to say, I'm tired of it."

"I never thought I'd say this about pizza," Josh said, "but me, too."

"How's the unpacking coming along?" Judy asked.

"We've got a long way to go," Sunday admitted. "We've spent most of the time since we got the keys painting." She quickly caught herself. "Not that there was anything wrong with the walls—we just wanted ..."

Judy held up her hand. "I can't remember the last time I painted the inside of this house. It's long overdue. I'm glad you could do it before you moved in."

"Would you like to see what we've done so far?" Sunday asked.

"Sure," Judy said.

"We chose a pale green for the kitchen." She gestured to

the surrounding room. "I love it with the cream-colored cabinets and charcoal gray countertops."

"It's a beautiful neutral palette," Judy agreed. "It goes with everything."

"That's what I told Josh," Sunday said. "He wasn't sure at first, but I convinced him we can change accent colors with the seasons and it'll be perfect."

"I agree with your wife," Joan said.

Josh just smiled.

Sunday led them from room to room. "The pale blue in our bedroom and master bath is called Sweet Dreams. Don't you love that name?"

"The name and the color," Judy said. "It's lovely."

"The rest of the rooms are done in a color called Toasted Coconut. I thought our dark wood furniture would look good against the walls, and our artwork would stand out. We'll eventually get rugs, too."

"What about the bedroom across from the master?" Judy asked. "Are you repainting that, or leaving it as is?"

Sunday and Josh glanced at each other.

"I'm afraid we ran out of energy and paint at the same time," he said.

"We'll use that room as a nursery," Sunday added, her cheeks coloring. "So we don't have to paint it right now, anyway. I'm taking next week off and will focus on unpacking."

"Graduation is Saturday," Josh said. "This is my last week as Maggie's assistant at Highpointe, and I still have several projects to wrap up before my replacement takes over."

"He starts his new job at Forever Friends the Monday after graduation," Sunday supplied.

"My goodness," Joan said, "you kids are busy."

"The place looks terrific," Judy said. "You're doing a great job with it."

"We'd like to have you and your husbands over for dinner once we're completely settled," Sunday said.

"That'll be very nice," Joan said as they ambled back to the front door. Dan and Cara followed along, tails wagging, as if determined to escort the visitors out.

"If you need tools—or advice on how to repair something —don't hesitate to ask Jeff," Judy said. "You may not know this, but he owned a hardware store back in the Midwest. When he moved to Westbury, I swear he brought half his inventory with him. If a tool exists, he has one."

Josh chuckled. "Good to know. I haven't done much home repair, but I'd like to learn."

"Jeff loves to teach," Judy said. "He'd be in his glory. Home repair and restoration are his thing."

They reached the front door. "Speaking of restoration," Sunday said, "do you know what's going on at the vacant mansion on the street behind here?"

Judy and Joan exchanged a glance.

"What are you talking about?" Judy asked.

"That vacant mansion. People have been in and out all week," Sunday said.

"I haven't noticed any changes," Judy said.

"I guess it looks the same from the front," Sunday agreed. "We've been hauling boxes and trash to the alley that runs behind both our properties," Josh said. "I've noticed a pickup truck going in and out of the back gate."

"Huh," Joan said.

"And I swear I saw lights—flashlights—from inside at dusk a couple of days ago," Sunday said. "I'll bet somebody's bought it and is fixing it up."

Judy glanced at her watch in an exaggerated fashion. "We'd better get going. Our husbands expected we'd be home ten minutes ago."

"Yes," Joan agreed quickly. "We told them we'd eat as soon as we got back."

Sunday pulled the door open. "We don't want to keep you. Thank you again for bringing us a home-cooked meal. I can't tell you how much we appreciate it."

"I hope you enjoy your supper," Judy said. "The only container I need back is the one with the chili."

"I'll wash it and leave it on your porch tomorrow," Sunday said.

"No rush," Judy replied.

She and Joan stepped onto the porch. Judy turned back to see Sunday and Josh, arms around each other's waists, framed in the doorway. Dan and Cara stood faithfully at their feet, watching the women depart.

"May happiness bless your days in your new home," Judy said softly, walking away with a contented heart.

CHAPTER 29

Gordon swiped to answer the call the moment his phone started buzzing. "Tim! How are you?"

"Things are great here, Gordon. I'm glad we finally connected. Sorry I couldn't get away from my meeting at Town Hall earlier. Your text said you're having dinner with your client tonight. I hope we don't have to cut this call short."

"Parisians dine late," Gordon said. "Eight o'clock. I don't have to leave for the restaurant for another hour, so we're fine. I'll let you take the floor—tell me everything that's going on."

"Sam and Jeff have completed as much work as they can without a dumpster on the property."

"Do you think we could sneak one in through the alley?" Gordon asked. "The back yard's like a jungle, if I remember correctly. We could hack out a spot for a dumpster that would be hidden from view."

"I'm afraid not, Gordon," Tim said. "A young couple who just moved in behind you noticed activity at the house and mentioned it to Joan and Judy."

"What is it about Westbury?" Gordon muttered. "Everyone knows everybody else's business."

Tim chuckled. "That's usually something we love about our town—but not always."

"So what did Joan and Judy say to these inquisitive neighbors?"

"They denied it, of course," Tim said. "But it proves my point. If you move forward with the restoration, people are going to find out."

Gordon was silent for a beat. "I hate to put Sam and Jeff on hold, but I'm not ready to go public yet. And I'd still like to enlist the help of a designer before I finalize my plans. Have you heard anything from Pam and Steve? You contacted them over two weeks ago."

"Steve got back to me late last night," Tim replied. "He apologized for the delay. Pam's mother died very unexpectedly the day after I emailed them."

"I'm so sorry to hear that," Gordon said.

"She was only sixty," Tim said quietly. "Apparently, it was an aortic aneurysm. Fine one minute—and gone the next."

"That's so young," Gordon murmured.

"Tell me about it," Tim replied. "My sixtieth birthday is already in the rearview mirror."

"What a tragedy," Gordon said. "That explains why we

haven't heard from them. I'm sure they'll be far too busy to take on my project."

"That's just it," Tim said. "Steve said they'd like to move forward. Pam's favorite thing is their TV show, *Wishes of Home*. They were in talks to syndicate it to a larger network when her mother passed. Irene had been their biggest cheerleader. She encouraged them to give up their personal training businesses and put everything into the show. She even told them, if it meant moving away from Linden Falls, they should do it."

"Were they going to?" Gordon asked.

"Steve said they had been considering it, but leaving her mom was always a sticking point for Pam."

Both men fell silent, neither wanting to voice the obvious.

"Anyway," Tim continued, "they need a splashy new project to clinch this network deal. They think your place could be it."

"I'm deeply sorry for the circumstances that made the decision easier for them," Gordon said, "but, aside from their sad plight, this is great news."

"Before committing and pitching it to the network, they want to meet you and see the house. I told them the house is available whenever they want, but I wasn't sure you'd be able to come back from Europe."

"I promised Anita I'd be in Westbury for the public hearing about the museum district," Gordon said. "She has ideas she wants to present, and I'll be in the audience cheering her on. She hasn't told me they've set a date yet."

"I can help with that," Tim said. "We just finalized it this morning. Three weeks from Tuesday, six p.m., in the council chambers. They'll post the notice this afternoon."

Gordon put the phone on speaker and scrolled through his digital calendar. "I can move things around and be there for the entire week. Will you contact Pam and Steve to ask if they can meet me then?"

"I'll do it as soon as we hang up, and I'll text you when I've talked to them. Steve said they met with Irene's lawyers and have almost finished cleaning out her house. They plan to put it on the market within the week. My sense is your timing will work out."

"That's perfect," Gordon said.

"If Pam and Steve want to feature the restoration on *Wishes of Home,* they'll want publicity—and your ownership will soon become common knowledge. You've guarded the secret so carefully," Tim said. "What do you need to do before you go public?"

Gordon sucked in a breath through his teeth. "I need to convince Anita Archer to come with me to Paris."

CHAPTER 30

A*listair*

We were hosting a baby shower—Susan's baby shower—and I couldn't have been more excited.

Maggie and John had gotten up extra early this Saturday morning. Instead of relaxing over coffee and the newspaper, they each filled their mugs, took a sip, and left their brews to grow cold while they hauled boxes in from the garage. These boxes had arrived at our front door during the past three weeks. I'm not sure why they bothered to carry them all the way to the garage, only to lug them back inside again, but nobody asked me.

I gathered this baby shower was not the sort of women-only gathering I was familiar with. Last night I snooped through Maggie's RSVP list—nearly as many men as women were attending. The one name missing was Julia's, and that made me sad. After all, she is going to be the big sister. I thought she should be there. I'd eavesdropped on Maggie's last phone call with Susan and learned Julia would be spending Sunday afternoon with her favorite babysitter—next to John, of course—Grace Acosta.

My humans had been gone longer than expected, so I went in search of them. I rounded the corner toward the kitchen door and almost collided with Roman and Eve. Their ears were down, and they tucked their tails tight between their legs. They met my eyes briefly and kept walking. I knew this body posture. Someone had been a bad dog. From the looks of things—a very bad dog.

I floated past them and joined Maggie and John on the back patio. Strange-looking clips, poles, and PVC pipe lay strewn across the brick pavers, surrounded by shards of busted latex balloons.

"I'm sorry, honey," John said. "I should've confined the dogs in the house."

"I guess they've never seen balloons before," Maggie said with a half-hearted laugh. "They sure had fun popping them."

"And with such speed and efficiency," John added. "Do we really need a balloon arch for the baby shower? I mean, I've never even heard of one before. Does anyone need a balloon arch for anything?"

Maggie put a hand on her hip. "They're all the rage right now—and they really are beautiful." She held up the photo from the kit they'd ordered online.

John squinted at the picture. "I'm not sure ours was ever going to look like that. A bunch of the parts we needed weren't included. But if you say we require a balloon arch, I'll go buy a new one. Where do they sell these things?"

"Online, I'm afraid." Maggie sighed. "We'll just have to make do with what we have."

I joined John in looking at the mess at his feet. Success seemed an unattainable goal to me as well.

John's cell phone chirped. He snatched it from his pocket, swiped to answer, and listened. "No, of course not, Sherry. You need to be with your sister. I'll come in and take care of the Saturday patients." He listened again, his expression softening. "I'll be there in ten minutes. I'm sorry about your sister. Don't worry about a thing."

He ended the call and turned to Maggie. "Unfortunately, sweetheart, I have to go to work. Sherry's sister is in the hospital, and she needs to care for her nieces and nephews this weekend." His words sounded apologetic, but his body language looked more like someone who'd just received a stay of execution from the governor.

Maggie glared at him.

"I have to go, sweetheart," he said. "A balloon arch isn't more important than the well-being of my patients."

Oh, John. Wrong line, wrong time. That last statement was not helping his cause. Of course Maggie knew he had to go, but, in my humble opinion, she had every right to be annoyed.

"How long do you think you'll be?" she asked.

"We're booked solid until closing at four, I'm afraid."

She nodded slowly. "Okay, then. I'll just figure all this out myself." The stiffness of her spine conveyed volumes.

I spun to John. *Please, please, please don't say something stupid,* I begged silently.

"I'll tell you what," John said, his eyes suddenly twinkling. "I'll send someone over to help you."

"Really? Like who?"

"I'm not sure yet," John admitted. "But I'll find someone. Help is on the way."

MAGGIE and I came in from the patio as soon as John left. She busied herself setting up the luncheon buffet on the dining room table. This was our usual warm-weather plan: guests would help themselves to food in the dining room and take their plates to tables on the patio. We kept six round tables for eight collapsed and stored in the garage, along with folding chairs. John had set them up when he got home from work last night.

Maggie was good at arranging plates, napkins, and silverware, and knew just how to stage the serving pieces and utensils—all with minimal direction from me. I grew bored and decided to check on my friends Roman and Eve. I wanted them to know that not everyone was mad at them.

They weren't in their baskets by the hearth in the library, so I headed upstairs toward Maggie and John's bedroom. But just then I heard a car pull up in front. I zoomed to the window on the stair landing, which afforded an unobstructed view of the driveway.

I inhaled so sharply at the sight that greeted me I nearly

knocked myself over. Alex Scanlon was getting out of his car and walking to our door. I returned to the first floor and hovered as the doorbell chimed through the house.

Maggie's slippers slapped the floor as she crossed the living room. She opened the door, her expression every bit as surprised as mine had been.

"Hi, Maggie," Alex said. "John called and said you needed help setting up for the shower for Susan and my brother tomorrow."

I hovered behind Maggie, almost able to feel the wheels spinning in her brain.

"It's so nice of you to come by," she said politely. Her tone was friendly, but her shoulders were tense. "I think I've got this."

"John said you'd say that—and told me I wasn't allowed to take no for an answer." Alex stepped across the threshold. He leaned slightly toward her as if to hug her, but straightened. "I understand our mission is to construct a balloon arch."

Maggie closed the door behind him and motioned with her head for him to follow. "Have you ever done one of these?"

"I'm not sure I even know what it is," he admitted. "But how hard can it be?"

She glanced over her shoulder. "That's what *I* thought—until I tried."

"For heaven's sake, Maggie," Alex said. "You and I worked together to find the people responsible for the fraud and corruption that almost bankrupted Westbury. If the two of us can do that, a balloon arch should be nothing."

They stepped out onto the patio. Maggie began sweeping up the broken balloon bits while Alex read the instructions and catalogued the materials.

"I estimate you only lost ten percent of the balloons," he said. "This kit was supposed to be ten feet long—so now it'll be nine. I don't think that's a big deal."

"I don't either," Maggie said. "Assuming we can decipher the instructions."

They set to work, and, before long, an impressive array of balloons in iridescent shades of white, yellow, blue, and green clustered into a generous arch that ended in a puddle of balloons at one side.

The three of us stepped back to admire their handiwork. I had to admit it was impressive. I was now a fan of balloon arches—words I never thought I'd utter in my afterlife.

"I'm glad you came by, Alex," Maggie said. "I don't think John and I would've done as good a job."

He smiled at her, then looked away.

"As you said—we make a good team, Alex."

"Do you need help with anything else, Maggie?"

She shook her head. "I've got it from here. You can get back to your busy Saturday." She started toward the kitchen door.

But Alex stood rooted to the spot. "There's something I'd like to talk to you about, Maggie. I was going to wait until Monday morning after the shower, but I think now is the right time."

She turned around and walked off the patio into the

sunshine. "I'd like to talk to you, too. I think we both need to clear the air about some things."

He nodded his agreement.

"Let's head down to the low wall in front of the woods."

Alex joined her, and they began walking.

"That's your special thinking spot, isn't it?" he asked. "I remember finding you there many times when we were unraveling the mess at Town Hall."

She smiled but kept walking.

They perched on the low wall and faced each other.

"Let me go first—please," Alex said.

Maggie gave him a thin-lipped smile.

"I assume you've heard about my idea to revitalize the town square with a museum district?"

"Fiona told me," Maggie replied. Alex cringed at the mention of Fiona's name. "I think it's a terrific idea," Maggie added.

"Then I guess you know I asked Fiona if she'd consider running the district?"

Maggie squared her shoulders. "She'd be a great choice. I just wish I'd have heard about it from you first, Alex."

Alex bit his lip and looked down at his hands. "I should have talked to you before I mentioned anything to her."

"It came at me out of left field," Maggie replied. "I was upset—I won't deny it."

"I shouldn't have run away from you after the groundbreaking."

"Why did you?"

They were finally talking things through. *Thank goodness.*

I hung back to give them space, observing as their body language shifted—from grand and dramatic, like debaters on a stage, to small and gentle, like old friends consoling one another. Slowly, the hurts and misunderstandings they'd both been carrying seemed to lift.

I turned my face to the sun and lay back, hovering as though floating in the ocean. I spend most of my time indoors, but today reminded me how pleasant it was to be outside.

CHAPTER 31

John snatched Maggie's cell phone from the kitchen counter and headed out the back door. He knew where he'd find her. He jogged down the sloping lawn, waving the phone over his head. "Aaron's calling!" he yelled.

"Answer it before it goes to voicemail!" she shouted back, jumping off the low wall and heading up the slope to meet him.

"Hey, Aaron," John said as he answered the call. Maggie joined him just in time to see the smile freeze on his face.

"Of course," John said. He tapped the screen to put the phone on speaker. "Maggie's just joined me."

"Hey, Mom," Aaron said. "Just calling to tell you we won't be at the shower."

"Very funny," Maggie said. "It's bad form for the expectant parents to ditch their own baby shower."

"We've got an ironclad excuse," Aaron replied. "Susan's water broke a few minutes ago. We're headed to the hospital instead of your house."

Maggie brought her hand to her heart. "Seriously?"

"I wouldn't tease about this," Aaron said. "I strapped Julia into her car seat, and now I'm going to help Susan out to the car. We'll drop Julia off on our way to the hospital."

Maggie and John heard a door opening in the background.

"I'm talking to your mom and John," Aaron told Susan, then switched his phone to speaker.

"Sorry, Mom," Susan said breathlessly.

"There's nothing to be sorry about," Maggie replied. "Mother Nature had other plans for you today. Have you got your hospital bag in the car?"

"I don't have one yet," Susan admitted. "I thought I had another month. We haven't gathered Julia's things either. And we don't know how long I'll be in labor, so Julia may have to stay with you tonight."

"Watch your head," Aaron said as he helped Susan into the passenger seat.

"Don't worry about a thing," Maggie said. "I'll come to your house, pack your bag, and bring it to the hospital. I'll get what Julia needs if she spends the night with us, too."

"Don't forget her Mousey," Susan said, referring to the stuffed mouse in a blue-and-white striped flannel nightgown that Julia always slept with.

"I won't," Maggie promised. "I know how important she is. We'd never get Julia to sleep without her."

The engine started. Susan groaned.

"Was that a contraction?" Maggie asked.

"Sure was," Susan said, her voice tight.

"How far apart are they?"

"They just started, so I'm not—" Another moan cut her off. "I guess that's our answer. They're pretty close together."

"Hey, Mom," Aaron broke in. "We were going to stop at your house to drop off Julia, but, considering how close these contractions are, would you mind coming to the hospital to pick her up?"

"We'll meet you there," Maggie said firmly. "Go straight to the hospital and leave everything else to us. The only thing you two need to do today is welcome your new baby into the family."

Maggie and John looked at each other, then sprinted up the lawn and into the house.

"I'm still in my PJs," Maggie said, racing up the stairs. "I'll throw on jeans and a T-shirt and be right down." She rejoined him in record time.

"I was thinking," John said as they headed to the garage. "Let's take two cars. I'll bring Julia back here and let the caterers in when they arrive with the food for the shower."

Maggie stopped short. "I think we should cancel the shower."

"Why?" John asked. "You've got everything set up already. It's too late to cancel the caterers. People will still want to drop off their gifts for Susan and Aaron, so the least we can do is give them lunch."

"You really think you can manage the shower on your own?"

"I didn't plan or set up everything," John admitted, "but I just have to put the food out and answer the door, right?"

Maggie bit her lip. "Well … you do have a point. There's no reason to waste all that food. I'll come home to help."

"You'll do no such thing," John said firmly. "Stay at the hospital with your daughter. I'll handle everything else. It'll be a breeze—food on the table, drinks on ice, smiles at the door. What could possibly go wrong?"

Maggie raised her eyebrows. She knew that kind of confidence was often the first step toward chaos. But she kept that thought to herself and let him have his moment.

JOHN CARRIED Julia into the kitchen at Rosemont. She clung to him, her face buried against his shoulder. "Did Mommy and Daddy get you out of bed before you were ready to wake up?"

He felt Julia's head move up and down.

"That's no fun," John said. "Would you like to go back to sleep now?"

She shook her head no.

"Look who's waiting to say hello to you." He turned his body halfway so she could see Roman and Eve sitting at his feet, their tails sweeping the floor. When he bent to put her down, Julia wailed and tightened her grip on his arm.

He straightened again. "Are you hungry?"

Again, she shook her head no.

Carrying her into the library, John sank onto the sofa. Cradling Julia against his chest, he leaned into the cushions, holding her and hoping she'd go back to sleep. Her deep, even breathing soon told him his wish had been granted.

The phone in his pocket vibrated. Carefully shifting his weight, he pulled out his phone and checked the message. The caterers would be at the door in under five minutes. John eased Julia onto the sofa, covering her with a light throw. The last thing he wanted was for her to wake to a ringing doorbell and barking dogs. He slipped out of the room and stepped onto the porch just as the catering van pulled up.

Two young men in black trousers and white smocks stepped out. John was heading toward them when a sudden cry from the library sent him back inside.

Julia came running, tears streaming down her face. "Mommy!" she wailed.

John scooped her up. "Mommy's fine," he soothed. "She and Daddy are at the hospital with your new baby brother or sister. We're having a big party today for your family." He attempted to set her down.

She protested and clung tighter.

"Julia," he said, soft but firm, "Grandpa needs to put you down for a few minutes. I have to talk to these men. Do you understand?"

She nodded reluctantly.

He set her on her feet, and she wrapped her arms around his leg instead. Dragging the sobbing child with him, John returned to the front door. One of the delivery men handed him an invoice.

John rubbed Julia's back while he scanned the document. His eyes widened. There were far more items than he had expected. He signed anyway.

"Where should we put this?" one man asked.

"On the kitchen counter, I guess," John replied.

The men carried in platters of sandwiches wrapped in plastic, three kinds of salad in large bowls, two foil-covered pans they handled with potholders, a tray of assorted cheeses, baskets of crackers, and a pink bakery box holding a sheet cake.

Still towing Julia, John followed them. "What do I do with these large pans with the foil on top?"

"You'll want to keep them warm until right before your guests arrive."

"How do I do that?"

"Put them in a low oven."

"What constitutes a low oven?"

One of the men walked over, set the oven to 200 degrees, and slid the pans inside.

"Do I need to stir them or anything?" John asked.

"No. The only trick is to remember they're in there. You'd be surprised how many people discover a whole dish left in the oven after the party."

"Got it. I won't forget." John glanced at the counter, now

crowded with food. "So I put all of this out in the dining room?" He gestured with his thumb.

The men stepped into the dining room. "Looks like you're serving buffet style. Someone has already laid out the dishes and serving pieces. That means you'll transfer the food from the disposable containers into your own serving dishes."

John blinked at the polished silver trays and crystal bowls Maggie had set out. "Transfer," he echoed weakly. "Okay, got it," John said more loudly, trying to sound confident. He gave a sheepish shrug. "My wife planned all this. She won't be here."

The two men exchanged a look.

"The mother-to-be went into labor early," John explained. "So Maggie's at the hospital. I've … taken over hosting the shower."

The right eye of one of the men twitched. "I'm sure everything will go fine," he said, though his doubtful glance slid to the clinging child.

"You've got your beverages handled, right?" the other asked.

John gave him a blank look.

"You know—ice in buckets, sodas, tea, wine? Everything's chilling?"

John's stomach dropped. Beverages. He hadn't thought of beverages. Not once. He forced a smile. "Oh, of course," he lied quickly. In his mind, he saw warm soda cans stacked in the pantry, and the lone ice cube tray in the freezer—half-empty and fused into one giant block.

"Enjoy your party," one man said, giving him a sympathetic smile as they walked out.

John closed the door. He stood in the foyer with Julia affixed to his leg.

"Alistair," he muttered. "I think I've bitten off more than I can chew. And if you really are out there, I wouldn't say no to your help."

CHAPTER 32

Alistair

He called my name!

I spun so fast I must have looked like a tornado. John was most definitely correct—he needed my help.

I had risen before either of them that morning. During my time as butler, I always got up before the family, especially on days like this when a party was on the schedule.

I had followed the morning's events closely. Maggie's decision to go to the hospital was, of course, the only sensible one. But continuing with the shower under John's supervision? Well, that seemed ... a stretch. His initial cockiness had alarmed me. I'd been putting my telepathic powers to the test, whispering to John that he needed my help. Evidently, I'd finally gotten through to him.

John stood in the foyer, Julia clinging to his leg like her life depended on it. Getting our girl calmed down and happy again was my first order of business. I spun to find Roman and Eve watching me, heads tilted, awaiting direction. Thank goodness we'd been communicating for years. I looked from them to Julia, then back again.

Roman swished his tail. Eve got to her feet, padded over, and rose on her hind legs. She planted her paws on John's leg and kissed the back of Julia's neck.

Julia giggled.

Roman joined in with his own kisses until Julia released John's leg and wrapped her arms around the dogs one by one.

"Right," John said, rubbing his hands together. "Can you come to the kitchen with Grandpa? I'll get you something to eat. I bet you're hungry."

Julia nodded and set off for the kitchen, with Roman and Eve trotting behind her.

John executed his one culinary skill—he made a peanut butter and jelly sandwich. He sat Julia at the table, set the sandwich and a glass of milk in front of her, and crouched to meet her eyes. "We're having a party later, Julia. Grandpa needs to make sure everything's ready. I'll be close by while you eat. Is that all right?"

She nodded again and took a big bite of her sandwich.

I steered John into the pantry, where cases of sodas and flavored iced teas were stacked.

"I'd better get these on ice," he said. "If I know Maggie, she's loaded bags of ice into the outside freezer."

He turned toward the garage, but I blocked his path.

"Right, right," he muttered. "I'll bring the beverage tubs into the kitchen first."

He lugged in four large silver tubs, filled them with cans and bottles, then fetched the ice. He dumped generous scoops over the drinks until the tubs sparkled with condensation.

Well done, John. I couldn't have done it better myself, I thought approvingly. This, of course, was not true. I could have done it better—far better—but encouragement seemed the wisest course.

Julia polished off her sandwich and carried her plate to the sink.

"I've still got work to do, sweetie," John told her. "Would you like to color a picture to give your parents when they come home from the hospital?"

She nodded.

John opened the cubby by the back door, pulled out a Disney princess coloring book and markers, and handed them to her. She scrambled back into her chair at the table and bent over her work.

John checked his watch. "Okay, Alistair," he muttered under his breath, "we've got forty-five minutes until people arrive. What now?"

Thank goodness he was listening. *Transfer the food to the serving pieces,* I thought at him as firmly as I could. The buffet was laid out in logical order. Cheeseboard first, then crackers, followed by salads, sandwiches, and the hot dish—an egg frittata, if I wasn't mistaken. The cake, of course, would come last.

John strode into the dining room and surveyed the credenza. "This makes sense. I can tell by the serving dishes and pieces what goes where." He headed for the kitchen, but I stuck out a foot to stop him.

He stumbled, caught himself, then nodded. "Better if I bring the serving dishes to the kitchen and transfer the food there, right? That way, if I make a mess, it's easier to clean up."

Bravo.

To my surprise, he proceeded with real dexterity. The buffet was perfectly set up minutes before the first guests arrived. I must confess, I had expected egg salad on the ceiling and crackers underfoot. John's competence came as a pleasant surprise. I convinced him to serve the warm dish just before the line formed.

"Anything else?" he asked, with a hint of bravado.

Roman and Eve bounded toward him.

"That's right," John said. "Let's take the two of you upstairs. You'll be happier there than underfoot down here."

Roman and Eve exchanged a doubtful glance. Happier upstairs? Their tails clearly said otherwise. But they were good sports, settling into their beds in Maggie and John's room.

We had just reached the bottom step when the doorbell rang. Julia ran to join John at the door and, to my delight, played the perfect hostess—smiling shyly and offering little waves as each guest entered.

Once everyone had a drink in hand, John raised his glass and tapped it with a knife. Conversation hushed.

"You've noticed the absence of three very important people," he began. "Maggie isn't here, and neither are Susan and Aaron. They're at the hospital because Susan went into labor this morning. So instead of a shower to celebrate the coming baby, with any luck, we'll be able to celebrate the actual baby."

A ripple of delighted murmurs ran through the crowd.

"Susan and Aaron want to thank you for your friendship, your caring, and your love," he continued. "Maggie and I want to celebrate the newest member of our family. Maggie arranged a wonderful lunch for all of us, so, without further ado, I invite you into the dining room to fill a plate. It's a beautiful day, and we've got tables on the patio, but please sit wherever you're comfortable."

"Have you had any updates from the hospital?" Sunday called to him.

John froze. I knew he hadn't checked his phone. We'd been too busy.

Not at the moment, I pushed at him.

"Not at the moment," John echoed smoothly. "But I'll keep you posted as soon as I hear anything."

I sighed in relief. For a man who had panicked over a low oven, he could deliver a toast with admirable grace.

CHAPTER 33

Maggie paced in the maternity waiting room, her cell phone clenched in her hand. When she'd arrived at the hospital, she'd gone straight to Susan's room. Her daughter had been in a great deal of pain, her contractions barely two minutes apart. Susan begged everyone around to find the anesthesiologist for her epidural. She'd clutched Aaron's hand so tightly that he grimaced.

The anesthesiologist arrived, and Maggie had kissed her daughter's damp forehead before slipping out to give them privacy. That had been three hours ago. Aaron had texted ninety minutes ago that everything was fine, and that Susan's labor had slowed.

Maggie checked her watch. The baby shower at Rosemont would be in full swing by now. She hoped John's confidence in himself was well-founded. Even if it wasn't, she reassured herself that Joan, Judy, Gloria, and the others knew the Rosemont kitchen as well as she did. If John needed help, they would step in.

She was gnawing her lip, pacing by the windows that overlooked the parking lot, when her phone rang.

"Aaron?" she answered breathlessly.

"It's me, Mom," Susan said. "Would you like to meet your grandson?"

"A boy?" Maggie's heart jumped. After three granddaughters, she now had a grandson. "I'm on my way!" She walked in to a sight that brought tears to her eyes. Susan lay propped up in bed, a red-faced infant swaddled against her chest. Aaron leaned over them, smiling as if his face might split from joy.

"Isn't he perfect?" Susan asked, never taking her eyes from her son.

"He certainly is. My goodness—look at that head of dark hair." Maggie glanced up at Aaron. "He gets that from you." She reached out to stroke the baby's cheek with a gentle finger. "I know he's four weeks early, but he doesn't look small."

"Seven pounds, three ounces," Aaron said proudly.

"That's a good size," Maggie replied.

"His lungs are fully developed, too," Aaron added.

"They think my due date was off," Susan said. "I didn't have a first-trimester ultrasound, so … who knows?"

"He's here, and he's healthy. That's all that matters," Maggie said, her voice soft with gratitude. "Have you picked out a name yet?"

Susan and Aaron exchanged a glance, then looked back at her.

"We have," Aaron said.

"Well?" Maggie teased. "Are you going to tell me—or is it a secret?"

"We want to tell you and John at the same time," Susan said. "We'd like to FaceTime with him."

"That's a great idea," Maggie agreed. "Except he's in the middle of your baby shower, remember?"

"You went ahead with that?" Susan asked in surprise.

"We thought, why not?" Maggie said. "We had all that food, and people had gifts they wanted to give you. So, yes."

"John managed it?" Susan asked.

"He did."

"Then I think it's the perfect time to FaceTime him," Susan said. "He can hold the phone up, and our friends and family can meet our son."

Maggie pulled her phone from her pocket.

"One thing first," Susan said. "Please comb my hair and put a little lipstick on me. You've got a tube in your purse, don't you?"

"Of course," Maggie said, fishing out her makeup bag.

"You don't need any of that," Aaron said tenderly. "You've never looked more beautiful."

"That's because I just gave birth to your son," Susan replied with a small smile. "Still, I want Mom to tidy me up a bit."

Maggie obliged, combing her daughter's hair and swiping a touch of lipstick across her lips. "There. And, for the record, I agree with Aaron—you've never looked more beautiful. Ready?"

Aaron and Susan nodded.

Maggie placed the call. John answered on the first ring.

"Have you got news?" he asked eagerly.

"We do," Maggie said. "Susan and Aaron would like to introduce their son to you."

"A boy?" John's voice was full of enthusiasm. "I can't wait to teach him all about sports."

"You'll have plenty of time for that," Maggie said. "Will you please gather everyone around the phone?"

"Sure." John held the phone away from his ear and gave a sharp whistle. "Everyone! Want to meet my new grandson?"

The guests clapped and cheered.

John climbed onto a chair, holding the phone high.

Alex and Marc pushed their way through the guests.

"The baby's uncle needs to have a bird's eye view," Sam said to the group, moving Alex into position directly in front of John.

"Can you see, Alex?" John asked.

"Sure can," Alex replied.

"Maggie's at the hospital," John said. "And she's going to turn the screen over to Aaron and Susan—and their new little boy."

"Hey, everybody," Aaron said, waving at the camera. "Thank you all for coming today. We're sorry we couldn't be there, but here's the reason why."

He stepped aside, and Maggie held the phone so the baby filled the screen.

"Meet *John Alex Scanlon,*" Aaron and Susan said together.

John's phone wobbled in his hands.

"Wait—what?" he blurted, gripping the phone tightly. "Did you say John? As in … me?" He looked around at the crowd, wide-eyed.

"Named after the best grandfather on God's green earth," Susan said.

"And the most wonderful brother a man could ask for," Aaron added.

John's throat worked as he tried to speak. "Well … uh … that's … wow." He jumped off the chair and he and Alex hugged, clapping each other on the back in congratulation.

The guests erupted in cheers and applause.

"I'll be home in a little while," Maggie told John as he focused the phone's camera at himself again. "Then you and Alex can come to the hospital to meet your namesake."

CHAPTER 34

The bell over the door at Archer's Bridal tinkled. Anita dragged her eyes from her computer and forced herself to get up. The shop had closed ten minutes earlier, and her staff had already gone home. She should have locked the door and flipped the sign to Closed. She hoped the customer wouldn't stay long—she wanted to continue preparing her presentation for the public hearing on Monday evening.

"Anita," a familiar voice called.

"Gordon!" She hurried out of her office and into his open arms. They kissed, and she pulled back to study him. "I didn't expect you until the weekend."

"I had to come in early for my meeting." He stopped abruptly, biting his lip.

"What meeting?" she asked. "You didn't tell me about it when we talked the day before yesterday."

"It just came up," he said. That part was true—Tim had arranged the meeting with Pam and Steve—but Gordon wouldn't tell Anita that. "With Frank Haynes and Josh Newlon, about Forever Guides."

"That's funny," Anita said. "I sat with Frank and Loretta at the baby shower on Sunday, and he didn't mention it. I talked to Josh, too, and he never said a word."

"Like I said, it just came up."

Anita tilted her head, studying him more closely. "Oh no. Is something wrong with the construction?"

"Not that I know of," he improvised. "I think they want to discuss changes to the plans."

"And that's an emergency?"

"It's better to make them now before construction is too far along." Gordon ran his finger under his collar. His white lies to Anita were piling up by the minute. "I came straight to you the minute I got into town. I'm still on Paris time—it feels like the wee hours of tomorrow to me. Let's grab an early dinner before I fall asleep."

Anita let the excuse slide, but unease pricked at her. Gordon looked tired, yes—but also evasive. She decided not to push further. "I'd love that," she said instead. "Do you mind if we stop by the museum first? I like to swing by after I close the shop, just to check that Fiona's crew has locked the doors and turned out the lights."

"Sure," Gordon said. "I haven't seen the dig site for weeks."

"A lot has changed," Anita said, grabbing her purse. "They've moved the still and the rolltop desk—basically everything except the mastodon—to the first floor for now. The pit is ten feet deep and takes up nearly the entire basement. The only other thing down there is the huge mound of dirt they've dug out."

They stepped onto the sidewalk, and Anita locked the shop door.

"That's because they have found so many bones," Gordon said. "It's exciting that it's such a complete skeleton."

"Fiona told me yesterday they've been searching for a week and haven't found anything else. She said they'd start filling the dirt back in today, so there may not be much to see."

Anita took his arm, and they crossed the square. The museum door stood ajar. They stepped inside. The basement door was open, and the murmur of voices floated up.

Gordon and Anita descended the stairs and paused at the bottom step. Fiona was on her hands and knees in the pit, flanked by a graduate student. From where they stood, only the top of her head was visible.

"Looks like they're still excavating," Gordon whispered.

"Hi, Fiona," Anita called.

"Oh, hey!" Fiona got to her feet and turned toward the stairs. "Gordon! Nice to see you." She climbed the ladder out of the pit. "Keep brushing the area where I was working," she told the student. "I know it may be wishful thinking, but I have a gut feeling we're going to find toe bones. It would be a shame to stop before we uncover them."

The student nodded and resumed brushing away dirt with careful strokes.

"You really think you'll find them?" Gordon asked.

Fiona shrugged. "Based on the condition and completeness of the other bones, I'm hopeful. Or maybe I simply want it so badly. It would be highly unusual. We've already got a more complete skeleton than the Warren and the Hyde Park Mastodons. Even the famous Burning Tree Mastodon—ninety to ninety-five percent complete—was missing all the toe bones and some tailbones. My competitive nature may be getting the best of me," she admitted with a grin, "but I want ours to be better than any of them."

"I don't blame you," Anita said. "Me too. I'm in no rush. Keep digging as long as you want."

"We've been at it for a week without uncovering anything new," Fiona said. "I think this—"

"Fiona!" the graduate student shouted from the pit.

Fiona, Gordon, and Anita turned to stare.

The student jumped to his feet. The look on his face told them what they wanted to hear.

"No!" Fiona cried, clutching her head with both hands and racing back to the pit.

The student nodded. "Come see for yourself. It's definitely a bone—and the right size and shape to be a toe."

Fiona scrambled down the ladder, dropped to her knees, and examined the discovery. "Yes!" she screamed, punching the air with both fists. She rocked back on her heels. The student pulled her to her feet and they high-fived, grinning ear to ear.

"What does this mean?" Anita asked from the steps.

"This guy may turn out to be the most complete mastodon skeleton in North America."

Gordon and Anita applauded as Fiona and the student climbed out of the pit.

"Do you mind if we work a little later tonight?" Fiona asked.

"Of course not," Anita said.

"I know I told you we'd fill the dirt back in by the end of the week," Fiona said. "But considering this find, we need to keep digging. I'm sorry, Anita."

"Don't be," Anita said warmly. "I'm thrilled."

"Thank you," Fiona said.

"Gordon and I are headed to Pete's for dinner." Anita paused and offered, "Would you like to join us—to celebrate?"

Fiona shook her head, smiling. "I'm hungry, but wild horses couldn't drag me away from here now."

"I figured you'd say that," Anita laughed. She and Gordon climbed the steps, and Fiona followed.

"Will you speak at the public hearing Monday night?" Anita asked.

Fiona nodded. "Maggie and I will make a joint presentation. I'll discuss the skeleton, and she'll talk about its community impact."

"I like the sound of that," Anita said. She glanced at Gordon. "I'll suggest other museums we could add to the district. I've been doing a lot of research—I think the district would be a powerful economic engine for Westbury."

"Wow," Fiona said. "That's terrific."

"I have one question about the mastodon," Anita said.

Fiona raised an eyebrow.

"If the council approves the district, I'd like the mastodon displayed there. I know I told Highpointe I'd donate it to them. Have you and Maggie talked about that?"

"We have," Fiona said. "She and I both agree this guy should be displayed in town."

"So the college agrees?"

"Maggie's working on it," Fiona said. "She's called a special meeting of the trustees. Displaying the skeleton at the college would be extremely expensive. There's no room for it in the geology building. They'd have to build a new facility, and Highpointe doesn't have the money. Maggie told me the trustees would need to raise the funds, and she doesn't think they'll be interested in doing that."

"I see," Anita said.

"Maggie wants to announce at the hearing that the college backs the museum district and the display of the skeleton there."

"That commitment should go a long way toward convincing the council," Gordon said.

"That's our hope," Fiona replied. She stretched, lacing her fingers above her head. "We'll put in another hour tonight and be back first thing in the morning."

"We'll let you get to it," Anita said. She and Gordon stepped onto the sidewalk.

"I've got an idea," Gordon said as they walked across the square to Pete's Bistro.

Anita raised an eyebrow.

"Let's send a couple of the daily specials over to Fiona and that student," he said. "She said they would only work for another hour, but I'd be amazed if they left there before midnight."

Anita squeezed his arm, touched by the thought—but her mind still snagged on the earlier conversation. Gordon was generous and kind, yes, but he was also hiding something. She could feel it.

"You, my dear, are a kind and generous man," she said aloud, smiling past her doubts.

CHAPTER 35

Maggie entered Pete's Bistro through the back door and made a beeline for the checkout counter. The hospital had released Susan and the baby the day before. Aaron had arranged for a replacement doctor to see his patients during the month after the baby was born, but he had scheduled everything based on the original due date. His replacement wasn't available a month early. Maggie had been more than happy to step in. She had quickly packed her overnight bag and settled in to help with Julia and the new baby. Other than preparing for her joint presentation with Fiona at the public hearing, she had left everything in Colleen's capable hands.

This afternoon had been chaotic, but Susan, Julia, and the baby were napping now. With a grocery delivery delayed until the next day, and nothing on hand for dinner, Maggie had placed a takeout order and dashed into town to pick it up.

The bartender handed her a paper receipt, her credit card, and a carrier bag loaded with containers. She thanked him and spun on her heel. With any luck, she would be back at Susan's before anyone stirred. The front door to the bistro opened, and a young couple stepped inside. Maggie stopped short, staring. She blinked several times, certain her eyes were deceiving her. But they weren't.

Pam Olson and Steve Turner—their friends from Linden Falls—had entered the restaurant.

The host led them to a table by the window. Maggie approached as they were sliding into their seats.

"Pam? Steve?"

"Maggie!" Pam cried. Both of them leapt to their feet.

Maggie leaned in for hugs, awkward with her purse slipping from her shoulder and the heavy carryout bag in her hand.

"What are you two doing in Westbury?" she asked.

"We're here scouting a location for the next season of *Wishes of Home*," Steve replied. "We arrived a few minutes ago."

"That's so exciting!" Maggie said. She looked from Steve to Pam, who remained quiet, her face pale and drawn.

"How long are you staying?"

"We're not sure," Steve said. "Our business here shouldn't take more than a day, but we thought it would be therapeutic to spend a few extra days."

Maggie set her carryout bag on the floor. Steve had a look of concern about him, and Pam was decidedly forlorn.

"I don't mean to pry," Maggie said gently, choosing her words with care. "Is everything all right?"

"You wouldn't have heard ..." Steve began, but Pam lifted her hand to stop him.

"My mother died six weeks ago."

Maggie gasped and pressed her hand to her lips.

"She had an aortic aneurysm," Pam said softly. "It came out of nowhere. She wasn't sick. I'm grateful she didn't suffer, but I'm still trying to wrap my mind around it."

Maggie pulled Pam into a tight hug. "What a terrible shock—for both of you." She looked at Steve standing behind Pam's shoulder. "I remember Irene from that day at the farmers' market. She was funny, kind, and so attentive to me and her other customers."

"She liked you too," Pam said, stepping back, her eyes shining.

"The table linens I bought from her are still my favorites," Maggie said.

Pam managed a small smile.

"Congratulations on another season of *Wishes of Home*," Maggie continued. "John and I have watched every episode—twice. And I'm glad you're going to spend a few extra days in Westbury. Time and space help with healing."

Pam nodded. "We both loved it here. Even if we hadn't come on business, we would've chosen Westbury as a place to get away."

"Where are you staying?" Maggie asked.

"We're at a business hotel along the highway," Steve said.

"Goodness gracious." Maggie shook her head. "That's not what you need right now. You'll want peace and quiet, nature and privacy. Come stay at Rosemont." She spoke firmly, as if she had already made the decision.

"We couldn't possibly impose," Pam said. Steve nodded.

"You wouldn't be imposing," Maggie said quickly. "In fact, you'd be doing us a favor. Susan and Aaron had their second child last Sunday, and I've moved in with them for the next week. The new vet John hired is out of town, so he's working ten-hour days. There's no one at the house—even the dogs are on their own. They'll be glad to have the company."

She leaned closer, placing a hand on each of their forearms. "You've been to Rosemont. You know there's plenty of room. And now you'll see it in summer. The back garden is peaceful, and the lawn slopes down to a wooded alley. I love sitting there with my coffee, listening to the birds and watching the squirrels. You'll have access to the kitchen if you want it. And don't worry about the dogs—we'll manage them."

She squeezed their arms. "Please come. I'd like to do this in honor of your mother. From what I know of Irene, this is exactly the kind of thing she would have done for my daughter if our situations were reversed."

Pam bit her lip and blinked back tears. "You're right about that."

"Do you remember how to get there from here?" Maggie asked.

Steve nodded.

Maggie fished her key ring from her purse, separated one key, and handed it to Steve. "Will you do the honors?"

"You're sure you want to give us your house key?" Steve asked.

"Yes," Maggie replied. "I need to get back to Susan's, and John won't be home for hours. Take the key and let yourselves in. We don't set the alarm. The dogs are friendly—it'll be fine."

Steve hesitated, then glanced at Pam.

She nodded, her voice thick. "Thank you, Maggie."

I'd better fly," Maggie said. "Settle yourselves into any guest room on the second floor. We've got plenty of coffee, and you're welcome to anything in the fridge or pantry. Make yourselves at home, and call me if you need anything. I'll let John know you'll be there when he gets home."

She pulled Pam into another hug, holding her tight. Neither woman spoke. Maggie finally stepped back. "Have a nice dinner, you two. John and I would love to catch up before you leave."

She picked up her carryout bag and slipped out the rear door.

CHAPTER 36

Alistair

After the commotion surrounding the shower on Sunday, Rosemont now felt like a seaside concession stand in the off-season—empty, forlorn, and quiet. My canine and feline friends were content to nap the days away. I was not.

With Sherry Parker still out of town, I knew John would be working long hours. Once Maggie had gone to help Susan and the children, I had resigned myself to solitude. I'd spent decades alone while Rosemont sat vacant, and I had gotten along fine. But I was no longer used to such silence. I didn't enjoy being solo anymore.

I busied myself in the attic, inventorying papers, checking the condition of stored furniture and artwork, and discouraging the mice and cockroaches by my very presence. Everything was neat, tidy, and in order. By Monday afternoon, the task was complete, and I prowled for something to do.

When Maggie, and later John, had first come to Rosemont, I had amused myself by playing hide-and-seek with their reading glasses, keys, grocery lists, and slippers. I would tuck them out of sight and watch with glee as the humans dashed up and down stairs, muttering in frustration. It was harmless fun, and, if I hid something too well, I always moved it to a spot where it would be "miraculously" found. But whether it was that I had outgrown such foolish games or because I had become so fond of them, the pastime no longer appealed to me.

By Tuesday, I had straightened every book on the library shelves and smoothed the fringe on the carpets. On Wednesday, I aimlessly drifted from room to room, feeling very sorry for myself. I was passing by the front door when a car pulled to a stop at the bottom of the steps. Another delivery, I thought, forcing myself up to the window on the staircase. A tall, dark-haired man and a very pretty woman—both in their thirties—got out. I was certain I'd seen them before, but couldn't recall where. They climbed the steps and disappeared from view.

A scratching sound in the lock sent me reeling back in shock. They had a key. These strangers were about to enter Rosemont.

I sped into the library and glared at Roman and Eve, who were still sound asleep in their baskets by the hearth. *What in the world is wrong with you? There are intruders at the door. This is your mission—your raison d'être—to bark at intruders!*

Roman opened one eye, Eve lifted her muzzle from her paws, and the front door swung open. Both dogs launched themselves forward, barking their fool heads off.

"Hey, guys!" the woman said, dropping to her knees and holding out her hands. "You remember us, don't you? Pam and Steve—we're friends of Maggie and John."

Eve stretched forward to sniff Pam's outstretched fingers. Steve joined Pam, and soon it was a full-fledged dog-and-human lovefest.

The woman's words jolted my memory. Of course! Pam and Steve had been with us this past Thanksgiving. They were the friends Maggie and John had made on their autumn holiday, when they'd helped shelter animals evacuated from the wildfire. Still, the fact remained: they had a key to Rosemont. I did not like it.

"I'll get our bags," Steve said.

Pam rose and wandered from room to room while Steve ferried in their luggage.

"This truly is a magnificent old house," Pam murmured. Her voice caught. "I wish … I wish my mom could have seen it. She would have loved it."

Steve put his arms around her and drew her close.

"I'm sorry," she said. "One minute I'm fine, and the next I feel shattered."

"There's nothing to apologize for," he whispered. "Losing your mother is huge. This is part of the healing process."

I straightened as if called to attention. Now I understood. Pam was deep in mourning, and Steve was grieving, too.

Maggie must have thought they needed Rosemont's peace in order to heal. Very well, then. I would do my part.

"Let's go pick out our room," Pam said, reaching for her carry-on.

"Don't worry about that. I'll bring everything up," Steve replied. "Let's decide where we want to put our stuff first."

They ascended the stairs with Roman and Eve trotting behind.

I knew exactly which room they should choose. It wasn't the largest, but it had the best view of the back garden. The curtains blocked the morning sun—valuable for a woman with dark circles under her eyes. And the claw-footed bathtub was the deepest in the house. A long soak would do her good.

Pam opened the door to the first guestroom—the one Susan often used. "Oh, my gosh," she breathed. "This has to be the most beautiful bedroom I've ever seen." She surveyed the room. "I don't think we need to look any further."

No, no, no, I thought. *Not this one. See the others.*

"Maybe," Steve said at last. "But I'd like to look at the others first."

They moved from room to room. "Each one is prettier than the last," Pam said, running her fingers through her hair. "Now I don't know which to choose."

"We've got one more," Steve said. "Let's check it out."

I held my breath as Pam opened the last door.

She stepped inside and slowly turned in a circle, taking in the soft cream, taupe, and robin's egg blue of the William Morris wallpaper. Blackout fabric lined the heavy cream damask curtains. A crocheted coverlet lay across the bed, and a bay window framed a cozy settee upholstered to match the wallpaper.

"This feels comforting," Pam said softly. She peeked into the bathroom. "Look at that tub. I can't wait to take a bath."

"Decision made?" Steve asked.

Pam nodded.

I did a little happy dance.

"I'll get the luggage," Steve said. "Go on—run that bath you were just talking about."

"Now?"

"You said you couldn't wait." He smiled at her. "We're on vacation. Take a bath whenever you want to. I'll even bring you the book you were reading on the plane."

She clasped her hands together. "That would be perfect. Reading in the tub is one of my favorite things."

"I'll be right back with your book," he said, heading downstairs.

I withdrew into the hallway and motioned for Roman and Eve to follow me. There would be plenty of time to play with Pam later. Right now, she needed one of Rosemont's greatest gifts: the magic of a healing bath.

As I drifted away, I felt the house itself stir with quiet purpose. Rosemont had always been more than timber and stone—it was refuge, solace, and sanctuary. The house would cradle them now. Grief was heavy, and Rosemont was strong enough to share the weight.

CHAPTER 37

Gordon waited on the back porch for the others to arrive. Sam and Jeff were to pick up Pam and Steve at Rosemont that morning, drive them past the front of the old house, and then slip through the alley to the rear gate. Concealed by overgrown landscaping, the property felt secretive—exactly what Gordon needed. He knew he couldn't keep his ownership hidden much longer. All he needed was a few more weeks.

The low rumble of Sam's truck announced their arrival. Gordon hurried to open the gate. Sam eased the vehicle under the sweeping branches of an old tree in the backyard and cut the engine.

Everyone piled out.

"Did you meet at the Rosemont Thanksgiving potluck?" Jeff asked, looking between Gordon, Pam, and Steve.

"We did," Gordon said, extending his hand. After warm

handshakes, he gestured to the house. "Thank you for traveling so far to see my ..." He paused, searching for the proper phrasing. "Declining relic."

"It's a beautiful home," Pam said, her gaze lingering on the silhouette of the historic home. "She's starved for attention, yes, but her bones are strong. The architect had a perfect eye for proportion and detail."

"That's exactly how I see her," Gordon admitted, flushing with pleasure. "Would you like to look inside?"

"Absolutely," Steve replied.

Gordon led the way to the back door. Steve paused on the bottom step, pushing aside an overgrown shrub. "This bit of foundation looks solid," he observed. "That's a good sign."

"We've done a structural assessment," Sam said. "She needs a new roof, new plumbing, and new wiring. But, otherwise, she's sound. I'll send you the inspection reports if the network wants to move forward."

"That would be very helpful," Steve responded. "We'll want to know exactly what we're getting into."

They stepped into the mudroom, and Gordon led them through the house—from the damp basement with its antiquated boiler to the dust-heavy attic filled with decades of forgotten things, and every room on the three floors between. Pam's pen raced across the pages of her brown spiral notebook, while Steve photographed each space from every angle.

By the time they returned to the first floor, the late-afternoon sun slanted through the windows, gilding the worn wood floors with honey-colored light.

"We understand you're not ready to disclose your ownership of this property," Steve said carefully.

"That's right," Gordon replied, his jaw tightening.

"We haven't said anything," Steve assured him. "But would it be okay if we took close-ups of the front façade? The network will want to see them."

"Are you interested in taking this on, then?" Gordon asked, his posture taut.

Pam and Steve exchanged a glance before nodding in unison.

"It's a larger project than anything we've done," Pam admitted, "but I think we're ready for the challenge. And I know our viewers will go wild over this place."

"If the network's game, so are we," Steve added.

Relief loosened Gordon's shoulders. "That's a big load off my mind."

"We can't guarantee the network will say yes," Steve cautioned.

"But how could they not?" Pam flung her arms wide. "Look at this place!"

Gordon chuckled. "The brush is too thick to walk around from the back. If you need those close-ups, you'll have to go out the front door."

"The porch is visible from the street," Sam said. "Are you sure?"

"If the network needs it, then yes," Gordon said firmly.

"I'll be quick," Steve promised. He adjusted the camera strap around his neck and stepped onto the front porch.

Pam lingered behind. "Do you know what style you'd like for the interior?"

"I want to honor the house's heritage and bones," Gordon said, "but I'm not a fan of heavy Victorian furnishings."

Pam smiled. "I'm glad to hear it. I'm not either. So—no fiddly wallpaper?"

"Definitely not. No wallpaper at all. These Venetian plaster walls shine on their own."

"What style of furniture appeals to you?"

"I'm an appraiser by profession and have developed a deep appreciation for both American and European antiques. I've been in France this summer, helping a client furnish a new home in London. While shopping for him, I've kept an eye out for pieces that would suit this house." He pulled out his phone. "Would you like to see what I've bought?"

"Of course," Pam said.

He handed her the phone. She scrolled through the photos, pausing and backtracking several times. "These are stunning," she said at last, lifting her gaze. "You have an excellent eye. And though they're not identical in style, they're cohesive. The proportions, the details—they connect beautifully. If you furnished the whole house this way, the look would be harmonious. Nothing would stick out."

"Thank you," Gordon said. "That's my goal—both for my client, and for myself."

"This makes me even more eager to work on your project," Pam said warmly. "I was already excited, but now I can picture it. Will you acquire more pieces while you're abroad?"

"Possibly." Gordon hesitated. "I don't plan to pick all the furnishings myself. There's ... someone else who will want a say. At least, I hope there is."

Pam opened her mouth to ask more, but Steve interrupted them when he burst through the front door, shutting it quickly behind him. "Someone was about to drive by," he said. "I wanted the door closed before they came into view."

"Good thinking," Gordon said.

Steve turned to Sam and Jeff. "Now for the big question. If the network approves this project and we decide to renovate this glorious old home for the next season of *Wishes of Home,* will you two manage our construction crew?"

"We were hoping you'd ask," Sam said. Jeff nodded.

"Excellent." Steve grinned. "Email me those inspection reports. We head back to Linden Falls a week from Saturday, and we've got a meeting with the network the following Monday. That'll give us time to put a proposal together."

"How long before they decide?" Gordon asked, his impatience plain. "I'm ready to move forward."

"Not long," Steve said. "We'll know sometime next week."

Pam touched the wall with reverence. "Here's hoping we can make your wishes for this home come true."

CHAPTER 38

David paced in front of the glass display cases, peering at the velvet trays of rings, watches, bracelets, earrings, and necklaces.

Harriet Burman stood on the other side of the cases. "Good morning," she said brightly. "Are you looking for something in particular?"

David shrugged. "I'm not sure. I've never bought jewelry before."

She gave him a thousand-watt smile. "Are you shopping for anyone in particular?"

He nodded but didn't elaborate.

Harriet had owned Burman Jewelers on the square with her husband Larry for over thirty years. She knew precisely how to help a customer like this.

"Is it for a woman or a man?" she asked.

"My girlfriend," David said at last. Then he hesitated. "Or at least … I think she's my girlfriend."

"Oh." Harriet's smile widened in encouragement. "So you're looking for something romantic, but not over the top. If it turns out you're still in the friend zone, you don't want to feel foolish."

David's nod was more vigorous this time. "A friend thinks she definitely likes me. Frank told me to come here to get a birthday present for her. A 'girlfriend' birthday present."

"That's good advice," Harriet said. "Sometimes our friends see things we don't."

"He's also older than me," David added quickly. "It's Frank Haynes. Do you know him?"

"Of course," Harriet said with a laugh. "Everyone knows Frank. He shops here often for special gifts for Loretta and the girls. If Frank thinks this girl likes you, I'll bet she does."

Relief flickered across David's face. "Okay, so … what should I buy her? I flew in this morning from California for a surprise birthday dinner tonight. Her mom invited me."

"Oh, that's a very good sign." Harriet leaned in, her tone warm. "If her mother invited you—especially since you'd have to fly in—then she knows you're important to her daughter." She tilted her head. "What is your budget?"

David told her the amount.

"You'll find something lovely for that," Harriet assured him. "Tell me, what kind of jewelry does she usually wear?"

David blinked. His blank stare was answer enough.

"Bracelets? Necklaces? Does she have pierced ears?" Harriet prompted.

He bit his lip.

"All three are popular," Harriet said kindly, "but, since you're not sure if her ears are pierced, we'll skip earrings. Some people don't care for bracelets, either. If this girl is sweet on you—and I think she is—she'll want to wear what you give her every day. I'd suggest a necklace."

She moved to another case, and David followed.

Harriet unlocked the case and drew out a velvet tray. "These are initial pendants," she explained. Delicate gold chains gleamed against the velvet, each strung with a letter. "We have two styles: simple block, or swirly script."

David bent over the tray. "I like the swirly ones. But her name is Grace, and I don't see a G."

Harriet opened a drawer, selected an italic G, and slipped it onto a fine gold chain. She placed it on the tray with care.

"That's pretty," David breathed. "I like that. Can I afford it?"

"Easily," Harriet said. "And you'd still have enough to add a small birthstone charm for only a little more. Her birthday is today, yes?"

"Yes."

"June has three birthstones," Harriet said, retrieving a tiny pearl charm. "The most popular is pearl." She fastened it to the chain beside the G.

David's eyes lit up. "That's really pretty. I think she'll like it."

"I'm sure she will," Harriet said warmly. "This is a very

special gift. You're a thoughtful young man, and she's a lucky girl."

David blushed crimson from collar to hairline.

"Would you like me to gift wrap it?" Harriet asked. "It's complimentary with every purchase."

"That'd be great," David said, handing over his debit card.

Harriet rang up the sale, returned his card, and studied him with grandmotherly kindness. "Have you bought a birthday card for her?"

David froze. "I didn't think of that."

"Why don't you pop across the square to Celebrations and pick one out?" Harriet suggested. "I'll shine the pendant and chain, and have the gift beautifully wrapped by the time you get back."

David exhaled, grateful. "Perfect. Thank you."

He stepped out into the sunshine, his pulse quickening. He needed to find a card that expressed how he felt about Grace.

CHAPTER 39

Judy took her mug and joined Anita at the small round table in the back room at Celebrations. The space doubled as a mail room, packaging center, inventory storage, coffee bar, and lunchroom. The two lifelong friends sat in bistro chairs, sipping café au lait from the fancy machine Jeff had given Judy for her birthday.

"This is delicious," Anita said. "What did you put in here?"

"A little splash of hazelnut creamer," Judy said. "Isn't it yummy?"

"Every bit as good as those fancy coffee drinks that cost a fortune."

Judy glanced around the cluttered space. "The atmosphere isn't as nice as a coffee shop."

"Nonsense," Anita replied. "I love tucking myself back here with you for coffee and a visit. How are you and Jeff?

What's he working on these days, now that the museum renovations are on hold?"

"He's been so busy," Judy said, leaning closer. "He and Sam might be hired for the next renovation project on *Wishes of Home*."

"The TV show?" Anita's hand flew to her chest. "Oh, my gosh—that's so exciting! They're coming to Westbury to film?"

Judy widened her eyes and pursed her lips.

"You know more than you're saying," Anita pressed. "What would they be doing in Westbury?"

Judy spread her hands. "I really don't know."

"Don't know—or can't say?"

Before Judy could answer, the bell above the shop door tinkled. She jumped to her feet. "I'd better get out there. Stay and finish your coffee. If you've got time, I'll make you another."

Anita drained her cup. "I have to get back to my shop anyway," Anita said, following Judy out front to find David entering the store.

"David!" Judy and Anita greeted him warmly.

"I assume you came in for the big meeting about Forever Guides yesterday," Anita said.

David frowned. "I flew in this morning. I don't know anything about a meeting concerning Forever Guides."

"The one to review construction changes," Anita clarified. "Gordon flew in for it and met with Frank at the site yesterday."

David shook his head. "I don't know anything about that.

Frank picked me up at the airport this morning and didn't mention it."

"Huh." Anita tilted her head, narrowing her eyes. "That's strange. Gordon told me about it in great detail last night at dinner."

Sensing tension, Judy stepped smoothly between them. "What can I help you with, David? I'm sure you're here for something in particular."

"I need a birthday card—for Grace Acosta," David said. His voice lifted with pride. "Her mom invited me to her surprise party tonight."

"How lovely," Judy said, steering him toward the card racks. "The birthday section is up front—funny, sentimental, and everything in between. I'm sure you'll find the perfect one. Do you have a gift already?"

"Yes," David said. "I bought her a necklace with her initial and her birthstone. Mrs. Burman's wrapping it now and suggested I come here for a card."

"You're in the right place," Judy said. "Take your time." She left him to browse and returned to Anita.

Her friend stood, staring into the distance. "Gordon's lying to me," Anita said flatly. "He didn't go to any meeting at Forever Guides yesterday."

"You don't know that," Judy said gently. "David wasn't in town, and maybe Frank didn't mention it because it wasn't a big deal."

"The way Gordon described it," Anita said, pain tightening her voice, "it was a big deal."

"If he did lie, he could have had a good reason," Judy said softly.

Anita leaned closer, her eyes bright with hurt. "If Gordon loves me, he shouldn't lie to me. Or perhaps I've been fooling myself. Maybe Gordon doesn't love me after all."

Judy gripped Anita's elbows. "You listen to me, Anita Archer. That man adores you. Don't you dare doubt him."

"You know something." Anita's voice dropped. "Don't you?"

Judy looked away.

"What is Gordon hiding? This isn't the first time. He lied before he went to Paris, too."

Judy swung back, her tone firm. "That's not for me to say. Just don't give up on that good man. As my mother would have said, he's a keeper."

Anita stepped back, blinking hard, and turned toward the door.

"Remember what I said," Judy called after her. "He loves you."

CHAPTER 40

David smoothed his shirt for the fifth time, leaned in, and pressed the doorbell. The living room window was open, and he heard sounds from inside.

"Grace, will you see who's at the door?" he heard her mother call. The slap of flip-flops echoed on the entryway tile. David held his breath as the doorknob clicked and turned.

Grace opened the door. For a beat she simply stared, astonishment painted across her face, and then it blossomed into pure delight.

"David!" she cried, launching herself at him and wrapping her arms around his shoulders.

He held her lightly at first, then drew her close. She tilted her head back, and when he bent to her, the memory of their long-ago embraces came rushing back. Their lips met, and they fused themselves in the kiss.

"David!" Grace's younger brother, Tommy, came skidding in from the kitchen.

Grace and David reluctantly pulled apart.

"What are you doing here?" Tommy demanded.

"Your mom invited me to Grace's birthday party," David said. "Didn't she tell you?"

Tommy shook his head. "Nope. I had no idea."

Grace's parents appeared in the entryway.

"I didn't even tell Kevin," Iris said with a grin. "The best way to keep a secret is to tell *no one*. The only other person who knew—besides David—was his mother. I called her to get your contact information."

Grace's eyes shimmered with tears. She swiped at a runaway drop with her fingertip. "We talk on the phone every day and text multiple times. I can't believe you didn't tell me," she said to David. "How long have you been planning this?"

David glanced at Iris. "Three or four weeks, maybe."

"That's a long time," Grace said, though her voice was soft with wonder.

Kevin stepped forward, shaking David's hand. "Nice to see you. And congratulations on keeping this a secret."

"You're right on time," Iris said briskly. "Dinner won't be on the table for another thirty minutes. I set out beverages and a charcuterie board on the patio for you two."

"Do you need my help, Mom?" Grace asked.

"Absolutely not. The birthday girl doesn't help with her own dinner. Your father and brother will assist me."

"Awww," Tommy groaned. "Don't we get snacks?"

"I saved some for us in the kitchen," Iris said, guiding him away. "Grace and David need time to catch up."

Grace laced her fingers through David's and led him through the dining room. A bouquet of balloons bobbed against the back of her chair; the family's silver and china gleamed on a fresh linen cloth; and a frosted birthday cake waited on the sideboard.

"Your mom goes all out," David said.

"She loves getting the 'good stuff' out for birthdays," Grace said with a fond smile. "Her mother and grandmother always used it for special occasions. She says it makes her feel close to them."

They stepped through the French doors onto the patio. A low table in front of the outdoor sofa held a charcuterie board of salami, brie topped with fig jam, nuts, and berries. A basket of crackers was next to it. An ice bucket of chilled beverages sat nearby.

"Would you like something to drink?" Grace asked, poking through the ice.

"In a minute," David said. The small, wrapped package from Burman Jewelers felt like an anvil in his pocket. "Do you mind if I give you your present first? While we're alone?"

"You didn't have to get me anything," she said, though her eyes telegraphed she was pleased he had.

He pulled the package from his pocket and thrust it toward her as if he were playing hot potato.

Grace perched on the sofa, and David sat beside her. She undid the wrappings, revealing a small velvet box. Her eyes flicked up to his, then back to the box.

"I hope it's okay," David mumbled.

She lifted the lid. "Oh." Her breath caught. She held up the delicate gold chain, the swirly G winking in the light, with the pearl charm nestled beside it. "It's beautiful."

David's heart thudded. "Do you … like it?"

Grace looked straight at him, eyes shining. "I love it." She leaned in and kissed him again. She handed him the chain, lifted her hair from her neck, and turned away from him. "Will you put it on me?"

David secured the clasp. He had survived the jewelry.

Grace turned back to him and noticed the envelope tucked beneath the box. She slid it open and read the simple line: *My world comes alive with happiness when I'm with you. Happy Birthday.*

Her smile shone so brightly the whole patio seemed to glow. "This means the world to me," she said softly.

David finally let out the breath he'd been holding since he stepped off the plane. For the first time, he believed Frank might be right. Maybe Grace did like him—really like him.

LATER, when the last of the cake plates had been cleared away, Tommy disappeared into his room to play video games, and Kevin and Iris settled into the family room to watch television. Grace and David slipped out onto the patio. Fireflies blinked on and off above the grass, tiny sparks of light dancing in the summer evening.

Grace leaned against him, her fingers tracing the necklace around her throat. "I still can't believe you flew in from California just for this," she said. "For me."

"I didn't have to think twice," he said. "I wanted to be here."

She turned toward him, smiling in that way that made his chest feel both heavy and impossibly light. "I'm glad you are."

They stood in easy silence, watching the fireflies' shifting glow. David felt something inside him settle—like the ground beneath his feet had finally stopped moving. For weeks, he had wondered if he was imagining things, if the hope he carried was only wishful thinking. But tonight, with Grace wearing his necklace and smiling at him like that, he felt certain they were back together.

"Happy birthday, Grace," he whispered.

"Best one yet," she whispered back.

CHAPTER 41

The Westbury town council chamber buzzed with conversation as people filed into the theater-style seating. Maggie and John slipped into seats in the back row.

"Anita and Gordon are up front," John said. "Looks like they've saved two seats for us. Do you want to join them?"

Maggie shook her head. "I'd like to sit back here to observe the audience. I'll be able to tell by body language how people are reacting to the ideas being presented. The museum district received the trustees' full backing. My mandate is to help convince the community. I'll modify my remarks to hammer home themes that I see resonate with the crowd."

"Great idea," John said. "You're a smart cookie. That's one of the many things I admire about you."

"I asked Alex to call on me last," Maggie said. "People fill out cards as they come in to indicate they want to speak.

Alex won't know how long the hearing will last until all the cards are collected. He anticipates a late finish."

"How late?" John asked.

"Until 10," Maggie said. "He'll call on me at 9:50. I know you've got to be at the animal hospital first thing tomorrow, so, if you want to leave early, that's fine. I'll get a ride home."

"And miss the presentation you've spent two days polishing?" John asked. "No way. I'm staying right here to cheer you on."

"Thank you," Maggie said, smiling. "You're the best husband. But if you change your mind, I'll understand."

She swiveled in her chair to watch people file in. "There's Josh and Sunday." She raised her hand in greeting.

Josh nodded, and he and Sunday claimed seats in front of them.

"Hello, you two," Maggie said, leaning forward. "Are you enjoying your new house?"

"We are," Josh said, "but settling in has been a lot. Sunday's run herself ragged."

Maggie studied Sunday's pale face and shadowed eyes. "Josh is right. You look exhausted."

Sunday blinked and gave a wan smile. "I'll be fine. I can't rest until everything's done."

"Tonight may run late," Maggie said gently. "If you get tired, don't hesitate to sneak out."

Before they could respond, Alex entered with the council members. He took his place at the center of the crescent-shaped council table and struck the gavel. The room hushed as people hurried to grab the last seats.

The evening began. Alex outlined the proposed museum district's structure, financing, and management. Then the city clerk drew the first speaker's card. A representative of the teachers' union spoke in favor of the district.

One by one, residents came forward. After an hour, John leaned toward Maggie. "We're running three to one in favor," he whispered.

She nodded. "That's my count, too. I had hoped for more support."

Anita's name was called. She strode to the podium and spoke with authority, precision, and persuasion—all without glancing at her notes.

"She's outstanding," Maggie whispered. Council members scribbled copious notes. "I think she's swayed the undecideds."

John nodded in agreement.

In front of them, Sunday slumped forward over her knees. Josh caught her, murmuring anxiously. Sunday nodded weakly and reached for her purse.

"She's not well," Josh whispered over his shoulder. "I'll take her home and come back for your presentation."

"You'll do no such thing," Maggie said firmly. "Go take care of her. You've already heard me rehearse. She needs you."

"Thanks," Josh said quietly. He and Sunday slipped out.

The stack of speaker cards dwindled. At 9:50, Alex rose. "As I said at the start, we'll conclude by 10. Thank you for your participation tonight. Our final speakers are Dr. Fiona

Locke of Highpointe College and former mayor and current president of Highpointe, Maggie Martin."

Maggie was already waiting in the aisle. She joined Fiona at the podium. Fiona spoke first, detailing the scientific significance of the mastodon. Then she gestured to Maggie.

"Thank you, Fiona," Maggie began. "And thank you, Mayor Scanlon, and members of the council, for giving the community this opportunity. This has been a most interesting evening. Others have already addressed many of the points I wanted to make. At this late hour, I won't repeat them."

"On behalf of the trustees of Highpointe College, however, I want to assure you of Highpointe's complete support for the proposed museum district. The college will lease one of the buildings and establish a natural history and science museum. As Anita shared, she is donating the mastodon skeleton to the college, and we will proudly display it there."

She turned to face the audience. "I've listened carefully to each of the speakers tonight. People have raised legitimate concerns, and we must address them. We can resolve every issue. This district isn't about ignoring problems—it's about solving them together."

Her gaze swept the rows, locking eyes with both skeptics and supporters. "What I see in this room is not division, but passion. Passion for our children, for our history, for our local businesses, and for the future of Westbury. A museum district can weave all of those threads together. It will be a place where our students learn, and our families gather with pride. Visitors will come to enjoy the museums, and shop and dine on the square. And it will honor our past and fuel our future."

"So I ask you, Westbury—not just as neighbors, but as stewards of this town—are we willing to invest in ourselves? To build something lasting for the next generation?" She lifted her arms, palms up. "What do you say, Westbury?" Maggie's voice rang out.

The chamber erupted in enthusiastic applause.

As Maggie made her way back up the aisle, Frank rose to shake her hand. "Masterful," he whispered. "If I were still on the council, I'd vote yes."

"Thank you, Frank," Maggie said warmly, continuing on as people reached out from the aisle seats to clasp her hand.

John stepped out to meet her. She pulled him with her toward the exit.

"Let's make a break for the parking garage," she said. "I don't want you to get stuck here longer than necessary."

"Not so fast," he replied with a grin. "After that state-of-the-union walk you just made, you're not slipping out. I'm sure Alex will want a word."

Maggie glanced back. Alex was already striding toward them. "You might be right," she admitted. "Alex will give me a ride." She kissed John's cheek and gave him a gentle shove. "Go on. Don't wait up."

Alex reached them. "Maggie, can I talk to you for a second?"

John eyed him. "Will you make sure that Maggie gets home safely?"

"Of course."

John moved toward the doors with the departing crowd.

"That gives me time to convince you of something," Alex said.

Maggie arched a brow. "Maybe I should have gone home with John after all."

"Too late," Alex said, taking her elbow. "You're mine until I drop you at Rosemont."

ALEX EASED the car up the winding drive and pulled to a stop at Rosemont's front door. The porch light glowed against the night, but the interior of the car was cloaked in shadow.

Maggie swiveled toward him. "You really want me to chair the citizens' advisory committee for the museum district—if it's approved?"

"After tonight, it's definitely going to be approved," Alex said. "And, yes, Maggie. We need you to chair it."

"I don't have time to assume a hands-on role in setting up the district," she protested.

"I'm not asking you to," Alex replied. "Westbury has a capable administrative staff. I've got my eye on a few people who could step into day-to-day management. We need someone with strategic skills and credibility who knows government and can unite people. Name me one person who fits the bill better than you."

"That's very flattering," Maggie said softly.

"The projects you thrive on let you leave a legacy of good.

You cleaned up fraud and corruption in Westbury. You've shepherded Highpointe College from a struggling liberal arts institution to one that's thriving and acclaimed. This museum district could be your next act."

Maggie drew in a slow breath. He heard the quickened rhythm of it—proof that she was intrigued.

"And if all that isn't enough," Alex added lightly, "you and I would work together again. What could be better than that?"

Maggie chuckled. "I have to admit, it's tempting. But I need to talk to John. This will affect him, too."

"Of course," Alex said. "There's no rush. Take your time."

"There is one thing I'd require," she said.

"Name it."

"I'd want the authority to appoint several members of the committee—and I'll insist on approving the rest. You know me well enough to trust I won't stack the deck with people who agree with me. Divergent viewpoints are necessary."

"I *do* know that," Alex said. "And the council does, too. That won't be a problem."

Maggie exhaled, her decision still hanging in the balance. She reached for the door handle. "I'll talk with John and get back to you by the end of the week." She pushed the door open, then glanced back with a faint smile. "And just so you know, Alex—working with you again would be the icing on the cake."

Alex's answering smile was warm and steady. "Likewise, Maggie."

Maggie nodded, the words settling comfortably between them.

CHAPTER 42

Alistair

I had not slept well. Maggie and John had left the house together right after an early dinner, but John returned home alone after ten o'clock. That was unusual enough to set me on edge.

At first, I thought Maggie had gone back to Susan's to help with Julia and the new baby. But Maggie had brought her overnight bag home Sunday afternoon, and I remembered her telling John that Susan's nanny was back in town and would be taking over for Maggie.

Twenty minutes after John's return, Maggie finally came in. She'd sat in a strange car out front for several minutes, talking to someone, before stepping inside.

I didn't know what to think. Had my happily married couple quarreled? The thought unsettled me more than I cared to admit.

Maggie took the dogs out, then went straight to bed, where John was already asleep.

I tried to make myself comfortable in my attic bed but eventually drifted down to the library sofa. I wanted to be on hand for any early morning conversations between the two of them—and I didn't trust myself not to oversleep in the quiet attic.

I tossed and turned the entire night but I needn't have worried.

John usually got up first, but it was different this morning. Maggie was already in the kitchen, waiting with fresh coffee and a steaming pot of homemade steel-cut oatmeal.

"Good morning," John said, clearly surprised. He crossed over to her and kissed her. "I'm amazed you're up. I didn't hear you come in last night."

"I wasn't far behind you," Maggie said. "Alex and I left shortly after you did."

John poured coffee, ladled oatmeal into a bowl, and sat. "Something's on your mind, isn't it? I can tell by your posture."

"If you're in a hurry to get to the animal hospital, it can wait," Maggie said.

"Oh boy," John replied. "Now I really want to know."

"Fair enough." Maggie's smile was thin. "Alex told me he's certain the town council will approve the museum district."

"That seemed obvious after your fabulous speech," John said.

Maggie turned off the burner under the oatmeal. "On the way home, Alex asked me to chair the citizens' advisory committee for the district." She looked directly at John. "What do you think about that?"

I drew near, finding it hard to believe what I was hearing. Hadn't they both spoken of slowing their lives down? Of taking more time for themselves, for hobbies—knitting, Mah Jongg—and for Rosemont? I had been dreaming of having them to myself more, not less.

John leaned back, thoughtful. "Sounds like an enormous commitment. Tell me more."

Maggie explained Alex's proposal. "I'd have flexibility," she said. "I could schedule my involvement around us."

Tell her it's too much, I urged silently. *Tell her to stay home.*

"Who would you ask to serve with you?" John asked.

I spun toward Maggie.

"Anita, of course," Maggie said. "She'd be essential. And Robert Harris—his tenure as rare books librarian at Cambridge would give us wonderful contacts. He has the right temperament for this."

I focused on John.

"He does. What about Frank Haynes?"

Back to Maggie. It was like I was watching a tennis match.

"He's busy with Forever Friends and Forever Guides," Maggie said.

"You know what they say," John countered. "If you need something done, ask a busy person. Frank has unmatched business acumen. I think you should consider him."

"You're right," Maggie narrowed her eyes, like she did when she was thinking. "I'd ask Frank, too."

I shrank back, watching them. This was going to happen. Maggie was already halfway to yes. Part of me swelled with pride, but another part sagged with disappointment. I had wanted quiet days at Rosemont with her, not something else that would take her away.

John set aside his mug and bowl and came to her, resting his hands on her forearms. He looked directly into her eyes. "I think you already know you want to do this. Alex is wise to have asked. No one else in town could fill this role as well as you."

"If I say yes," Maggie asked, "do I have your blessing?"

"Without a doubt," John said. "You've got plenty of time for hobbies later. This could be another exciting chapter in your life."

I swallowed the lump in my throat. I needed to stop thinking about myself. If this was what Maggie wanted, then I was happy for her. She would go on doing remarkable things for Westbury. My role was to support her in whatever she chose.

Maggie and John went their separate ways, and I padded back into the library. Roman cracked one eye at me; Eve lifted her head, ears twitching. "Yes, yes," I told them both. "Our Maggie is off to conquer Westbury yet again." I lowered myself onto the sofa with a sigh. "I do wish she would conquer knitting needles instead. Less glory for her, perhaps, but far more time for us." Roman huffed, Eve tucked her nose under her paw, and I resigned myself to sharing my Maggie with yet another grand endeavor.

CHAPTER 43

Sunday sat at the kitchen table, her hands wrapped around a mug of chamomile tea. A sleeve of saltines rested beside her, with one cracker half-eaten on the napkin at her elbow.

Josh walked in, heading toward the coffeemaker, but stopped short when he saw her. "Are you still feeling sick?"

She gave the faintest nod, as though even that slight movement took effort.

He pressed the start button on the coffeemaker and slid into the chair across from her. "I'm so sorry. I heard you get up for your shower this morning and thought going to bed early last night had done the trick."

Sunday managed a wan smile.

"You must have a stomach bug. Or food poisoning?"

"No," she whispered. "I haven't thrown up. I'm just … incredibly nauseated."

"Are you going to call in sick?"

"I hope this tea and a few crackers will settle things," she said. "I plan to go to work."

"Do you want me to stay home with you?"

"Of course not," Sunday said. "This is your last week as Maggie's admin. You don't want to miss it."

"It'll be fine," Josh said. "Colleen's a quick study—she's already taken over all of my duties."

"That's great," Sunday said. She lifted the mug and took a careful sip. "But you should still go in. Today is Tuesday and graduation's Friday. You've loved this job. Don't miss the ending."

Josh hesitated, then rose to fill his thermal mug. "Text me, okay? Let me know if you make it to work or if you decide to take a sick day."

"Okay."

"I'll stop at the store on the way home to pick up something for dinner. Chicken noodle soup is usually a good choice for an upset stomach."

"I'll let you know this afternoon," she said.

He crossed back to her, brushing a kiss over the top of her head. "I'll grab anything else you need. I don't know if we have any Pepto or Alka-Seltzer in the house."

"I don't think those will help," Sunday said quietly, as he started toward the door. Then, almost as an afterthought, "But you might want to pick up a home pregnancy test."

Josh froze, hand on the doorknob. He let it drop, turned, and crossed the kitchen in two strides. A slow, disbelieving smile spread across his face. "Really?"

"I can't be sure," she said, meeting his gaze. "But this doesn't feel like any stomach bug I've ever had. And … I'm late. Which never happens."

He furrowed his brow, calculating.

"We may be celebrating our first Valentine's Day in this house as a family of three," Sunday said softly. She searched his face. "I know this is sooner than we planned. Are you … pleased?"

His arms came around her instantly, drawing her against him.

She buried her face in his neck.

"This is the best news I've ever had," he said thickly. "Better even than finding my birth parents. Better than the day you said yes. To hell with our plans—we'll make it work."

"We may have to turn that spare bedroom into a nursery sooner than we thought," she murmured.

"I can't wait to buy the paint and get started," he replied.

He bent to kiss her, but she pulled back with a small laugh. "Not right now. I'm too nauseous. Leave me to my crackers and tea."

He squeezed her shoulder, smiling, then picked up his coffee. "I'll see you tonight." At the door, he turned back to her. "Whether we are or we aren't—I adore you."

CHAPTER 44

Several blocks away, on the other side of the square, Anita and Gordon sat at her kitchen table nursing their morning coffee.

"Your presentation turned the tide," Gordon said.

"I don't know about that," Anita replied.

"I do. I watched the council the entire time you were speaking. Three of them started taking copious notes about thirty seconds in. I'm certain you changed minds."

"I hope you're right."

"Be proud of yourself," he continued. "Your speech was informative, well-researched, and persuasive. I think you'll be swamped with calls today congratulating you." His eyes twinkled. "In fact, I'll bet museum-district business will keep you so busy that you won't get anything done at the bridal shop."

"We're not that busy right now," Anita said. "And my

workroom supervisor is back today. It won't matter. What's on your schedule?"

"I'll be knee-deep in phone calls and emails myself."

"For your client in France?"

"He's still away for another ten days. But I've had a sudden flurry of work for a client in New York."

"Then I'd better let you get to it." Anita pushed back her chair.

Gordon reached for her hand. "Before you go ..." He hesitated, then drew a deep breath. "I want you to come to Paris with me when I leave on Thursday."

"As in the day after tomorrow?" Anita asked, pulling her hand back.

He nodded. "You just said the shop isn't busy, and your supervisor is back. Fiona's still working on the dig, so Sam and Jeff can't move forward with the final renovations of your museum. My Paris client is out for ten days. It's the perfect time for us to get away."

"But I'd have to get ready."

"That should be easy. You have a passport. Pack a bag, and we're off. If you forget something, we'll buy it in Paris." He leaned forward, earnest.

Anita turned her face aside. "There's something else, Gordon. I've dreaded saying this, but I can't go to Paris with you until it's resolved."

He straightened. "Go on."

"I know you've been lying to me."

His eyes widened, but he said nothing.

"Several people have seen you around town, but, when

they've mentioned it to you, you've denied it. You told me you ate the sandwich I brought you—but I found most of it in my trash. These may seem small to you, but they aren't to me. I need to trust the man I've fallen in love with."

"Anita . . ." His voice faltered.

"Don't deny it. I can give you specifics, if you want."

He lifted a hand in a stop sign gesture. "No need. You're right. I did lie."

She pressed back into her chair.

"But not for nefarious reasons," he added quickly.

"So, there are good reasons to lie?"

"Yes. Sometimes."

"Then tell me what's going on."

"That's why I want you to come to Paris with me. I planned to explain everything there."

"That's asking a lot. Why not tell me here and now?"

He held her gaze while the grandfather clock ticked loudly in the hallway. "I love you. I'd never do anything to dishonor you. You know that."

"That was true—until you started lying."

"Don't I deserve the benefit of the doubt?" he pressed. "I canceled my trip to return to Westbury when the mastodon was discovered and flew back from Paris for the public hearing. I've made you my top priority. All I'm asking is that you trust me enough to let me explain in my own way."

Anita pressed her lips into a thin line.

"You don't have to decide right now," Gordon said. He reached into his satchel and pulled out a slim envelope. "I never dreamed you'd say no. Our tickets are in here." He removed two tickets and slid them across the table. "The first gets you from Westbury to JFK. The second takes us from JFK to Paris."

Anita tilted her head, studying him.

"I'll leave your tickets with you." He rose, poured the rest of his coffee down the sink, and set his mug in the dishwasher. "I've said all I intend to say—for now. Think about it."

"Where will you go?" Anita asked.

"Back to New York. I have work to do. But I'll be on that flight Thursday." He slung his satchel over his shoulder and strode toward the door.

"But, Gordon," she called after him, following. "I only want the truth."

He spun back. "And I'm offering it. You want someone you can trust. *I* want someone who has confidence in me—not someone quick to jump to the wrong conclusion."

He opened the door and stepped outside. "I'll be heartbroken if you don't join me, Anita," he said quietly. Then he turned and walked away.

CHAPTER 45

Maggie stepped into Archer's Bridal and smiled at the woman who greeted her. Recognizing the woman, Maggie said, "Dolores, good to see you again. Is Anita in?"

"Yes, Maggie, she's in her office. Always a pleasure to see you," the woman replied, waving her through.

Anita sat at her desk, back to the door, staring out the window to the parking lot behind the shop.

"Good morning," Maggie said. "I wanted to congratulate you on your presentation last night. It was absolutely brilliant—you set the museum district firmly on the path toward approval."

Anita swiveled her chair around.

"Good heavens, Anita—you look positively bereft. Haven't you been flooded with calls and emails praising you?"

"It's not that." Anita's expression remained glum. "People have been kind—" she gestured toward her computer. "I've received at least a dozen emails already. But that's not why you're here." She motioned toward the empty chair across from her desk.

"I also came by to ask you something," Maggie continued, still standing and studying Anita. "It's a beautiful day. Too nice to spend inside. Why don't we walk over to the square?"

Anita got slowly to her feet. "Good idea. I could use a change of scenery."

They crossed the street without speaking, the silence heavy around them.

Maggie pointed to a shaded bench beneath a canopy of leaves. "When I was mayor, I used to sit here to think through problems."

"Do you think I have a problem?" Anita asked.

"Something's troubling you," Maggie replied.

They sat. Anita leaned back against the bench, turning toward her friend.

"Let me start with why I came to see you," Maggie began. "As you know, the public hearing demonstrated considerable backing for the museum district," Maggie said. "Alex gave me a ride home afterward and told me the town council will approve it at their next meeting. Thanks in no small part to your presentation, Anita. Everyone was impressed with your vision."

"I'm excited about it," Anita replied, though her voice was flat.

"Alex said the council will form a citizens' advisory

council to ensure continued community input. He doesn't want a rubber-stamp group—he wants guidance."

"That's good to hear," Anita said, a flicker of enthusiasm returning.

"Alex asked me to chair the new group," Maggie continued. "I told him I'd do it—on one condition. That I'd be able to choose three members myself. And the first person I'm asking is you."

Anita blinked. "Me? Maggie, I've never served on a council or committee in my life. I don't know what I'd contribute."

"Reread the speech you gave last night, and you'll see," Maggie said firmly. "I told Alex I wouldn't serve unless you agreed to be part of it."

Anita pressed a hand to her chest. "If you truly want me . . ."

"I do."

"Then, yes. I'd be honored."

"That's wonderful," Maggie said, smiling. "We'll do important work together. And it'll be fun."

For the first time that morning, Anita smiled. "This makes me feel a teeny bit better."

"What's weighing you down?" Maggie asked. "Do you want to talk about it?"

Anita sighed. "Gordon invited me to spend next week with him in Paris." Her eyes turned solemn. "We're supposed to leave the day after tomorrow."

Maggie frowned. "That wonderful man who's head over

heels for you—who you clearly feel the same about—wants to take you to Paris? And that's a problem?"

"Yes—because Gordon has been lying to me."

"Oh, surely not."

"I confronted him this morning. He admitted it."

"Did he explain why?"

"No. He said he'd tell me in Paris."

"Well, that sounds romantic to me," Maggie said.

"I need a man I can depend on. One who doesn't lie."

"Mmm." Maggie studied her. "I know Gordon better than anyone in this town. He's the poster child of dependable. His integrity is unwavering. And he's extraordinarily kind. I think you owe it to him—and to yourself—to hear what he has to say."

"What if I get there, and his explanation isn't good enough? I'll be heartbroken."

"The way you looked when I walked into your office—I'd say you're already heartbroken," Maggie said softly. "All your friends know the two of you are crazy about each other."

"Judy said the same thing," Anita admitted. "But why won't he tell me here?"

"I don't know," Maggie said. "But he's promised to explain in Paris. I think you should go and find out. Who knows—this might be the best week of your life."

CHAPTER 46

The rideshare driver placed Anita's luggage on the curb, wished her a pleasant trip, and drove away. Extending the handles, she rolled her suitcase and carry-on to curbside check-in. At just after 5:00 a.m., the airport was deserted. The attendant checked her bag and handed her the claim slip.

Inside, the terminal was hushed, with only a handful of travelers moving past shuttered newsstands. Coffee bars were beginning to open, the scent of roasted beans drifting into the air. Anita silently scolded herself for arriving so early. She had gone to bed before eight, tossed and turned the entire night, and finally given up on sleep a little before three. By four, she'd called for the rideshare. She didn't know if her restlessness came from her fear of flying—or the thought of seeing Gordon again.

She paused at a bank of monitors, found her flight

number, and breathed easier when she saw *On Time* flashing beside it. With her carry-on bumping behind her, she headed through security, then straight to her gate. She was the first one there.

Choosing a seat at the far end of a row, away from the counter, Anita pulled out her book club novel. Judy had warned her the story was slow to start, but worth it—and Judy was right. Anita was soon so absorbed that she barely noticed the gate area filling around her.

It wasn't until a little boy tripped on her bag, toppling it over, that she looked up and realized passengers were already lining up to board. Flustered, she shoved her book into her carry-on and hurried to join the line. She had meant to text Gordon earlier, but now she promised herself she'd do it once she was seated on the plane.

The gate agent scanned her first-class ticket, and Anita walked down the jetway.

"Welcome aboard," the flight attendant said warmly, reaching for her bag.

"I'd like to get a few things out first," Anita replied. "It isn't heavy—I can manage."

"Of course. Just let me know if you change your mind."

Anita unzipped the outer compartment, pulled out her purse and book, then slid the carry-on into the overhead. She settled into her aisle seat just as the man with the window seat next to her arrived. She stood to let him in, then tucked her book into the seat pocket and reached into her purse for her phone.

Her stomach dropped.

The purse was small, accommodating just a wallet, a makeup pouch, mints, and glasses case. She pulled each item out, one by one. And dug her fingers into every corner. She checked the zippered pouch where she kept tissues and a card with emergency contacts and her allergies. No phone.

Heat crept up her neck. Had it slipped into the carry-on when she'd shoved her purse inside? She glanced at the overhead bin, but the aisle was jammed with boarding passengers. Anita moaned.

"Excuse me, ma'am?"

She turned toward her seatmate.

"Are you all right?"

Her throat tightened. To her own dismay, tears filled her eyes. "I think I've lost my phone."

"That's unfortunate," he said, his tone kind. "I've done that before." He offered a small, reassuring smile. "Don't worry. When we land at JFK, you can replace it. If you know your carrier login, they'll freeze your old phone and transfer your number. Even your data, usually. It's a hassle, but not a disaster."

Anita blinked hard, willing herself to be calm. "It's just … I really needed my phone right now. I'm meeting someone in New York. I want him to know I'm on my way."

The man studied her for a moment, then reached into his pocket. He unlocked his phone and held it out. "Please. Use mine."

"You're sure?" she asked, hesitant.

"Of course. We all need a favor from a fellow traveler now and then."

Her fingers flew across the screen as she typed:

On my way, darling. See you at JFK. I love you. — A

ANITA CLUTCHED THE AIRSICKNESS BAG, praying she wouldn't need it. The flight had been miserable. Turbulence had rattled them almost the entire way. Except for one hurried trip down the aisle to toss miniature bags of pretzels at the passengers, the flight attendants had been strapped into their seats, looking as queasy as everyone else.

The captain had apologized more than once, explaining that they couldn't seem to find calm air. Now he came on again, confirming what every passenger with a watch already knew: their arrival was delayed by more than an hour.

A flight attendant's voice filled the cabin, briskly rattling off connecting flight numbers and their departing gates. Anita leaned forward, straining to hear. When she caught her own flight number, she scribbled the gate down on her boarding pass.

"We'll be on the ground in ten minutes," the attendant finished.

Anita groaned. She had never been to JFK before, but she knew the airport's reputation—arrivals and departures were rarely close together.

"Where's your connection leaving from?" the man beside her asked.

She told him.

"Good thing you're in first class," he said. "As soon as we

stop at the gate, stand up, grab your suitcase, and line up at the door. I know this airport like the back of my hand. If you hurry, you'll make it."

Anita swallowed hard, fighting both her nausea and the rising panic in her chest. She managed a grateful nod. "Thanks."

CHAPTER 47

Gordon checked his messages for what felt like the hundredth time that morning. Nothing from Anita. He jerked back into his seat, rubbing a hand across his eyes. She wasn't coming.

He couldn't believe it. He'd been so sure she would join him. But clearly, he didn't know her as well as he thought he did. He exhaled, heavy and resigned, and switched his phone into airplane mode before shoving it into his pocket. Was this the end for them? His heart felt like it had broken into a million pieces. He needed time to think.

A flight attendant appeared with a polished smile. "Would you like something to drink, sir? Perhaps some champagne to celebrate going to Paris?"

He shook his head, waving her off. "I'm not celebrating," he muttered under his breath.

She moved on. Moments later, he heard her announce

that the doors would soon close—that this was the last chance for passengers to order a drink before takeoff.

Gordon shoved the complimentary headphones on and began scrolling the touchscreen, searching for something to distract him from his misery.

Then the same attendant rushed past his seat, returning with another passenger in tow.

"You're right here, next to this gentleman," she said.

Gordon yanked off his headphones, irritation prickling. He turned toward the aisle, ready to object—the attendant was referring to the seat he'd purchased for Anita—only to have the words freeze on his lips.

Anita stood before him. Her face was flushed and hair disheveled, and her chest heaved as she gasped for breath, looking like a runner who had just staggered across the finish line of a hundred-meter dash.

Gordon shot to his feet, stepped into the aisle, and pulled her into his arms. He kissed her as if they were the only two people on earth.

Applause broke out around them.

Flustered but beaming, Gordon tucked her carry-on into the overhead, then guided her into the seat beside him.

The flight attendant reappeared, this time with two flutes of champagne. "I overheard what you said a few moments ago, sir. I believe you now have something to celebrate."

Anita laughed breathlessly as she accepted a glass. "I made it. I didn't think I would." She sipped, then told him about the lost phone, the delayed flight, and her mad dash through JFK.

"That's why I didn't hear from you," Gordon said.

"I borrowed the phone from the man next to me to text you. Didn't you get it?"

Gordon drew a slow breath. "My phone blocks unknown numbers. It must have gone straight to spam."

Anita laid her hand over his. "You thought I wasn't coming, didn't you?"

He nodded, and the pain of it showed in his eyes.

"I'm so sorry you had to go through that," she whispered.

"You're here now," Gordon said. "And that's all that matters." He raised his glass, his gaze never leaving hers. "To us—and to our Paris adventure."

CHAPTER 48

"We're here, sweetheart," Gordon murmured in her ear.

Anita opened her eyes and lifted her head from his shoulder. "Did I fall asleep?"

He nodded, smiling. "One minute you were pointing out the beautiful stone buildings with their wrought-iron balconies from the window of our cab, and the next you were out cold."

"I barely slept the night before we left," she said. "And I don't think I got a wink on the plane."

He opened the taxi door, stepped onto the pavement, and extended a hand to her.

"Jet lag is real," he said. "It knocks me flat every time. I never plan much for my first day in Paris."

She slid across the seat and joined him on the sidewalk. "Gosh, this looks fancy," she said, glancing first at the medallion inlaid with the hotel's name beneath her feet, then up at the elegant façade rising five stories above them.

The driver unloaded their luggage and passed it to the waiting bellman.

"Are we staying here?" Anita's voice expressed her delight.

"We are. We've got a suite overlooking the Tuileries Garden, right across the street. This neighborhood—the Rue de Rivoli in the 1st Arrondissement—is perfect for a first visit. We're close to the historic sites, shops, cafés ... everything."

Inside, the lobby was small but refined, with gilt-framed mirrors and polished marble floors. Gordon led Anita into a cozy sitting room where they served croissants and coffee in the morning and tea and hors d'oeuvres in the afternoon. Silver trays of cheeses and crackers beckoned.

"Why don't you relax here while I check us in?"

She sank into a citrine-yellow silk armchair. "Thank you."

It was nearly twenty minutes before Gordon returned with the room key. Anita had dozed off again, chin resting on her chest. For the second time that afternoon, he coaxed her awake.

"Let's get you upstairs. I think someone needs a nap before dinner."

They squeezed into the tiny elevator, with only enough room for them to stand shoulder to shoulder.

"Good thing it's only the two of us in here," Anita said.

"People built these older hotels for stairs," Gordon replied. "The bellman must get his exercise."

The elevator groaned its way to the third floor, stopping with a bounce. Gordon led her to a door halfway down the hall and unlocked it.

Anita stepped inside, taking in the sitting room with its full sofa, two armchairs, a desk, and an armoire that doubled as a coffee station. A basket of fruit, nuts, and chocolates sat on the table, but she walked straight past them to the tall French doors. She turned the gilded handle, pulled the doors open, and stepped onto the narrow balcony.

She stopped, speechless.

"It's magnificent, isn't it?" Gordon said, joining her.

"More than magnificent." She pointed. "That's the Eiffel Tower. And that huge, tree-filled space right across the street —you said that's the Tuileries Garden?"

He nodded. "It's a formal French garden, with long gravel paths, rows of manicured trees, statues tucked into green alcoves, and fountains where Parisians sit and read."

Her gaze shifted to the vast building stretching beyond the garden. "And that's the Louvre. It's even bigger than I imagined."

"Enormous—and it used to be larger. The Tuileries Palace once connected to the Louvre, but it burned in an uprising in 1871. The Louvre became a public museum during the French Revolution. Today it's the largest museum in the world."

Anita leaned on the balcony railing, taking it in. "All right across the street. The building itself is stunning."

Gordon put his arm around her waist and nodded toward the horizon. "The Seine runs just beyond the Tuileries. Place

Vendôme and the Paris Opera House are behind us. And the Musée d'Orsay—see the building with the great round clocks?—that's just over the river."

Anita tore her eyes from the view and turned to him. "It's overwhelming. Beautiful. I can hardly believe I'm really here."

Gordon inhaled slowly. "Would you like to have our talk now?"

She shook her head. "Not yet. I'm too tired—I'd rather wait until I'm clear-headed."

"Would you like to nap for a couple of hours? We'll go to dinner when you wake up."

"What time is it?"

"Just after five."

She wrinkled her nose. "If I nap now, I'll zonk out for hours."

"Dinner here runs late. Eight to eleven is normal. You'll have plenty of time."

She laughed. "That's so different from home. Instead of sleeping, could we walk around the neighborhood a little, grab something to eat, and go to bed early? I promise I'll be better company tomorrow."

"That sounds perfect," Gordon said. "And to be honest, I'm beat, too. I don't think I'd last until eight either. There's a famous tearoom halfway down the block—Angelina. The front desk can arrange for us to skip the line. They're famous for their hot chocolate and croissants."

Anita's eyes lit up. "Angelina? The place Coco Chanel

went every afternoon for hot chocolate? She would dunk a croissant in it."

He grinned. "That's the one."

"I've read everything I can about Chanel, Dior, Balenciaga —all of them. I've wanted to go there for years. And I want to dunk a croissant in my hot chocolate."

"We'll both do it," he chuckled. "Now's the perfect time," Gordon said. He slipped an arm around her waist and drew her close. "But before we go, there's one thing I've been waiting for since the day I booked this room."

"What's that?" she asked.

"I've wanted to kiss you on this balcony."

She melted into his arms, and, for a while, all thoughts of Paris, museums, and fashion icons gave way to the quiet wonder of being exactly where she was meant to be.

CHAPTER 49

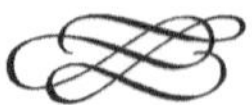

Hand in hand, Anita and Gordon stepped out of the hotel and onto the Rue de Rivoli. The early morning light gilded the cream-colored façades, making every wrought-iron balcony and carved cornice shimmer.

Anita slowed, her gaze darting everywhere at once. "Even the sidewalks feel elegant," she murmured, glancing at the shops tucked beneath the stone arches.

Gordon smiled at her wonder. "This is the Paris I wanted you to see first—alive but not overwhelming. Most shops won't open for hours. The best way to see the city is simply to walk and let it surprise you around every corner."

Across the wide boulevard, the Tuileries Garden stretched out in a sweep of manicured green. Beyond the treetops, the Louvre's glass pyramid caught the sunlight.

Anita squeezed Gordon's hand. "I feel like I've stepped

into a painting. Everything is more beautiful than I imagined."

"Lead the way," he said.

"Me? I don't know where anything is—you should be the guide."

"There's no wrong direction in Paris. We'll see wonders whichever way we go. We'll purchase timed tickets for the Louvre and Versailles for later in our visit, but today—let's wander where your intuition takes us."

She cast him a dubious glance. "Okay. After that breakfast we just ate in the hotel's restaurant, I'd like to walk some calories off. I don't want to go home ten pounds heavier."

"You won't," Gordon promised. "We'll be logging twelve to fifteen thousand steps a day."

They strolled two blocks, then crossed the boulevard and circled the Louvre's vast exterior. When they reached the Pont du Carrousel, Anita turned to him. "Can we go across the bridge? Is there much to see on the other side?"

"Oh yes," he replied. "Quite a lot."

They walked on, hands swinging between them.

"I've seen lovers strolling across Paris bridges in films," Anita murmured. "I never thought I'd get to do it myself."

Their steps carried them past the Musée d'Orsay, its giant clocks gleaming, and the domed Institut de France. By midday, they stood before the newly restored Notre Dame, its pale stone glowing and stained-glass windows brilliant in the sun.

"Can we come back and tour this?" Anita asked.

"Of course. Do you want to go inside Notre Dame now?"

She eyed the long queue snaking toward the security checkpoint. "I think I'm fading. You were right about all the walking."

Gordon checked his smartwatch. "Care to guess?"

"Ten thousand?"

"Twelve thousand, five hundred thirty-four," he said with a grin.

"No wonder I'm tired."

"Let's cross the Seine, grab lunch from a boulangerie, and picnic in the Tuileries."

Her face lit. "Perfect."

They collected a warm baguette, a large chicken and leek quiche, and a peach tart. From the wine shop next door, they bought a bottle of red. The tart's sweet fragrance accompanied them into the garden.

Gordon led Anita away from the bustle at the octagonal Grand Basin, where children sailed colorful toy boats. They found a worn stone bench shaded by trees, both private and connected to the lively scene around them.

"This feels tucked away," Anita said, settling beside him.

Gordon uncorked the wine, poured it into two plastic cups, and handed one to her. "I'll let you tell me when you're ready to talk."

Anita took a sip, watching an elderly couple amble by arm in arm. She turned back to Gordon. "How about now? I'm ready."

His fingers brushed the small box in his pocket. He drew in a breath. "I've rehearsed this in my head a dozen times. It's complicated. I'll answer every question you have—just let me finish first."

She arched her eyebrows, then nodded.

"I made a big purchase in Westbury," Gordon began. "A house. An old one, in need of serious restoration. It wasn't even on the market—I had to persuade the owners to sell. Alex saw me exiting the parking garage after signing the papers at the law firm, and I've been meeting with Sam and Jeff about the restoration work."

"For heaven's sake, Gordon—why wouldn't you—"

He lifted a hand. "Not yet. Let me finish. I didn't buy it for me."

Her confusion deepened.

"It's the house behind the square—the one you've told me a dozen times is your favorite in all the world. I bought it for us."

She gasped.

He pulled a small box from his pocket and removed a key ring with an old-fashioned iron key. Dropping to one knee, he looked into her eyes.

"This isn't a typical ring for this moment, and I'll get you any ring you'd like, but I wanted to start with this. Anita Archer, I've loved you since the moment I met you. I believed love at first sight was sentimental nonsense until I met you. You are kind, compassionate, funny, adventurous—and you encourage me, you understand me, and I know that you love me. Will you marry me?"

Anita slipped the keyring onto the ring finger of her left

hand and flung her arms around his neck, pulling him back onto the bench. "Of course I'll marry you, Gordon."

Their kiss was long and slow. When they parted, both dabbed at damp eyes with paper napkins from the boulangerie.

"I'm so sorry I doubted you," Anita whispered. "I fell for you on that horrible drive back from the small appliance museum. You were so kind and encouraging to me. My sewing machine museum was your idea. You *are* trustworthy and your integrity *is* without question."

"Maybe I should have told you sooner," Gordon said. "But then I dreamed up this proposal—here, in Paris, with the key to the house you've always wanted. To keep the surprise, I had to keep the secret."

Anita shook her head, smiling through tears. "I still can't believe it. What a . . ." she paused, turning the key ring around on her finger, "unique proposal. I can't wait to tell Judy and Maggie about it. They were on your side, by the way. They insisted I come to Paris."

"I'm glad to know they were in my corner."

"I can't believe you bought us that house! Tell me about the renovations."

He described his meetings with Sam and Jeff, and the involvement of Pam and Steve.

"You mean we might be on *Wishes of Home*?" she cried.

"If you're comfortable with it. I told them the decision was yours."

"Consider me comfortable," Anita said, twisting the keyring around her finger.

"I've also bought a few furnishings while shopping for my client," Gordon continued. "They're stored here in Paris—I want you to see them. If you don't like something I've picked out, I'll resell it. We'll shop together for more, too."

"I feel like a Victorian heroine," Anita said, laughing softly. "Couples used to travel to Europe to furnish their estates."

"That's exactly what we're doing. And speaking of shopping, Paris has more jewelers than you can count. Tomorrow, I want you to choose your engagement ring."

Anita pressed her hand to her cheek, shaking her head slowly. "I can't believe this is real."

Gordon grinned. "So it wasn't the worst proposal of all time? I hear social media is full of scripted productions these days."

Anita cupped his face in her hands. "Gordon Mortimer, this is the most romantic, dreamiest proposal ever. If it were posted on social media, it would go viral."

They kissed again, lingering and unselfconscious. In Paris, lovers on a park bench were simply part of the landscape.

THE END

THANK YOU FOR READING

If you enjoyed *Love and Legacy,* I'd be grateful if you wrote a review.

Just a few lines on Amazon or Goodreads would be great. Reviews are the best gift an author can receive. They encourage us when they're good, help us improve our next book when they're not, and help other readers make informed choices when purchasing books. Goodreads reviews help readers find new books. Reviews on Amazon keep the Amazon algorithms humming and are the most helpful aide in selling books! Thank you.

To post a review on Amazon:

1. Go to the product detail page for *Love and Legacy* on Amazon.com.
2. Click "Write a customer review" in the Customer Reviews section.

3. Write your review and click Submit.

In gratitude,

Barbara Hinske

JUST FOR YOU—MAGGIE'S DIARY

Wonder what Maggie was thinking when the book ended? Exclusively for readers who finished *Threads of Kindness,* take a look at Maggie's Diary Entry for that day at https://barbarahinske.com/maggies-diary.

ENJOY THIS EXCERPT FROM GUIDING EMILY

Prologue

Emily. The woman who would become everything to me. The person I would eat every meal with and lie down next to every night—for the rest of my days.

She was just ahead; behind that door at the far end of the long hall. I glanced over my shoulder. Mark kept pace, slightly behind me. I could feel his excitement. It matched my own.

Everyone said Emily and I would be perfect for each other. I'd overheard them talking when they thought I was asleep. I spend a lot of time with my eyes closed, but I don't sleep much. They didn't know that.

"A magical match," they'd all agreed.

I lifted my eyes to Mark, and he nodded his encouragement. I gave a brief shake of my head. Only four more doorways between Emily and me.

I picked up my pace. A cylindrical orange object on the carpet in the third doorway from the end caught my eye. *Is that a Cheeto? A Crunchy Cheeto? I love Crunchy Cheetos.*

I tore my eyes away.

This was no time to get distracted.

We sped across the remaining distance to the doorway at the end of the hall. The door that separated me from my destiny.

I froze and waited while Mark knocked.

I heard Emily's voice—the sound I would come to love above all others—say, "Come in."

What was that in her voice? Eagerness—anxiety—maybe even a touch of fear? I'd take care of all of that right away.

The door swung open and Mark stepped back. He pointed to Emily.

I'd seen her before. Emily Main was a beautiful young woman in her late twenties. Auburn hair cascaded around her shoulders and shone like a new penny. With my jet-black coloring, we'd make a striking couple.

"Go on," Mark said.

I abandoned all my training—all sense of decorum—and raced to her.

Emily reached for me and flung her arms around my neck.

I placed my nose against her throat, and she tumbled out of her chair onto her knees.

I swept my tongue over her cheek, tasting the saltiness of her tears.

"Oh … Garth." My name on her lips came out in a hoarse whisper.

I wagged my tail so hard that we both lay back on the floor.

"Good boy, Garth!"

She rubbed the ridge of my skull behind my ears in a way that would become one of my favorite things in the whole wide world.

Next to food.

Especially Crunchy Cheetos.

Mark and the other trainers were right—we were made for each other. I was the perfect guide dog for Emily Main.

Chapter 1

"Weren't you supposed to leave for the airport half an hour ago?" Michael Ward asked his boss, whose fingers were typing furiously on her keyboard. "You're still planning to get married, aren't you?"

Emily Main's head bobbed behind the computer, her eyes fixed to the screen.

"I can't believe you put off a departure to Fiji to help us launch this new program. Your wedding's in two days."

"We've been working on this for almost a year. I wasn't about to leave when we're this close. I just need to finish this last email." She hunched forward and peered at the computer screen.

"There," she said, pushing her office chair back as the email *whooshed* from her inbox. "Done."

She looked up at Michael, blinking. It was probably the

first time she had looked at anything besides a computer screen in hours. "I brought my suitcase so I could go to the airport straight from the office. I don't have to stop at home."

Michael raised his eyebrows at her. "That's all you've got? A carry-on and a satchel for a week—a week that includes your wedding? My wife packs more than that for a three-day weekend."

"My wedding dress is a classic sheath and the rest is bathing suits and shorts."

"I would have thought Connor Harrington the third would have wanted an elaborate wedding—one fit for the society pages."

"Our wedding is going to be very elegant—think JFK Junior and Carolyn," Emily said, flinging her purse over her shoulder and reaching for the retractable handle of her suitcase.

Michael stepped in front of her. "I've got this," he said. "I'll walk you to the street. I'd like to congratulate Connor on snagging our office hero."

Emily hesitated.

"He is picking you up, isn't he? You're flying there together?"

"He went out over the weekend. He wanted to do some diving with his best man ... sort of a bachelor party reprise. I was traveling with my mom and maid of honor, but they flew out yesterday as planned. The company paid to change my ticket, but it would have cost almost five hundred dollars for Mom and Gina to change theirs. It wasn't worth it."

"But you don't like to fly." He peered into Emily's face.

"Did you talk to Connor about that before you decided to stay an extra day? You have told him about your fear of flying, haven't you?"

Emily shrugged. "I've mentioned it, sure, but I haven't made a big deal out of it."

"So what did he say?"

"He suggested that I get a prescription for Xanax and sleep the whole way out there."

"Really? That's what he said?"

"He's a Brit, for heaven's sake. 'Stiff upper lip' and all that. He's not the sort of guy to coddle anyone—and I'm not a needy type of gal. You know that."

Michael cocked his head to one side. "Do you have to change planes?"

Emily nodded.

"You don't want to be knocked out for that."

"I'll be fine." Emily threw her shoulders back. "You don't need to worry about me."

"I know—I'm sorry. It's just that I wouldn't let my wife make the trip alone if she felt like you do about flying."

"I fly alone all the time, and nothing's ever happened to me. There's no reason this time should be any different."

Michael lifted his hands, palms facing her, and shrugged. "Okay, but I think he could have at least offered to pay to change your mom's flight or something."

"I'll be perfectly fine." Emily walked past him into the hallway. "I promised Dhruv that I'd say goodbye before I leave."

"He's going to miss you. You're the one person here that really connects with him."

Michael watched her shoulders sag slightly.

"Hey," he said, rolling the carry-on to a halt beside her in the hall. "I'm sorry. I didn't mean to worry you. The whole team is going to step into your shoes while you're gone. We've talked about it."

"Of course you will. I shouldn't worry about him. I've got the best team in San Francisco. Scratch that. On the entire West Coast." Emily gave him a teary smile and punched him playfully on the shoulder. "I know you'll take care of everything while I'm away, Michael—including helping Dhruv stay connected with the team."

"Good!" Michael continued down the hallway. "I don't want you to give this place a second thought while you're gone. If anyone deserves a vacation—and a gorgeous beach wedding—it's you, Em. But don't get too comfortable." Michael turned and smiled at her. "We do need you to come back. We'd be lost without you here."

Emily laughed and pushed him toward the elevator. "Why don't you go push that button, you wonderful suck-up. It'll take ages to get an elevator this time of the morning. I'll stick my head into Dhruv's cubicle and be right back."

***

Emily found Dhruv, as usual, leaning into the bank of computer monitors, intently focused on the complex strings of code in front of him. She cleared her throat.

When Dhruv didn't move, she tapped him lightly on the shoulder.

Dhruv sat back quickly and spun around. A smile spread across his face when he saw her.

"I wanted to say goodbye before I go."

Dhruv nodded. "Goodbye."

"I'll see you a week from Monday."

"I know. You're getting married in two days, then you have your honeymoon for a week, then you come back to work," he recited.

"That's right. You remembered."

"I remember things."

"Yes, you do. That's one reason you're so very good at programming," she said.

"I know."

"Okay … well … have a good week. You can go to Michael if you have … if you need anything."

"I know."

Emily regarded the shy, socially awkward middle-aged man who was, by far, the most proficient member of her extremely talented team of programmers. "Bye."

Dhruv nodded.

Emily stepped away.

Dhruv leapt out of his chair and called after her. "Have a happy wedding."

Emily swung around and gave him a thumbs-up then turned back toward the elevators where Michael was waiting.

From *Guiding Emily*

ACKNOWLEDGMENTS

I'm blessed with the wisdom and support of many kind and generous people. I want to thank the most supportive and delightful group of champions an author could hope for:

My remarkable husband, Brian Willis, who never fails to support me;

My life coach Mat Boggs for your wisdom and guidance;

My kind and generous legal team, Kenneth Kleinberg, Esq., and Michael McCarthy—thank you for believing in my vision;

The professional "dream team" of my editors Linden Gross, Dione Benson, and proofreader Dana Lee;

Elizabeth Mackey for a beautiful cover.

RECURRING CHARACTERS

Recurring Characters in the Rosemont Series

· *Rosemont and the Martins*

- **Maggie Martin Allen** – current owner of Rosemont; president of Highpointe College; former forensic accountant and mayor of Westbury; widow of Paul Martin; married to John Allen; mother of Mike Martin and Susan (Martin) Scanlon; grandmother to Julia and John Alex, and twins Sophie and Sarah Martin
- **John Allen** – veterinarian; owner of Westbury Animal Hospital; Maggie's husband; "adopted grandfather" to Julia, John Alex, Sophie, and Sarah
- **Paul Martin (deceased)** – Maggie's first husband; disgraced former college president; father of Mike and Susan; affair with Loretta Nash, father of Nicole

- **Mike Martin** – Maggie's son; lives in California with wife Amy and twin daughters Sophie and Sarah
- **Amy Martin** – Mike's wife; mother to Sophie and Sarah
- **Sophie and Sarah Martin** – twin daughters of Mike and Amy; close friends of Marissa Nash
- **Susan Martin Scanlon** – Maggie's daughter; attorney at her brother-in-law's firm; kidney donor to half-sister Nicole Nash; married to Aaron Scanlon; mother to Julia and John Alex
- **Hector Martin (deceased)** – town patriarch; son of Silas, father of illegitimate son (Frank's father); donated rare book collection to Highpointe College
- **Silas Martin (deceased)** – Hector's father; amassed fortune from sawmill and real estate; built Rosemont
- *At Rosemont*
- **Alistair** – Rosemont's longtime butler; now a loyal and witty ghost in the attic

- *The Scanlons*
- **Aaron Scanlon** – orthopedic surgeon; married to Susan Martin; father of Julia and John Alex
- **Alex Scanlon** – Aaron's brother; attorney; succeeded Maggie as mayor; partner of Marc Benson
- **Julia Scanlon** – daughter of Susan and Aaron
- **Marc Benson** – musician; Alex Scanlon's partner
- **John Alex Scanlon** – son of Susan and Aaron

- *The Acostas*
  - **Grace Acosta** – David Wheeler's girlfriend; babysitter for Scanlons
  - **Tommy Acosta** – Grace's younger brother; befriended Nicole Nash and David Wheeler while hospitalized
  - **Iris Acosta** – mother of Grace and Tommy; married to Kevin
  - **Kevin Acosta** – professor at Highpointe College

- *The Nashes and Hayneses*
  - **Loretta Nash Haynes** – former mistress of Paul Martin; married to Frank Haynes; mother to Marissa, Nicole, Sean (with Paul); later children Bonnie and Branson with Frank
  - **Marissa Nash** – Loretta's oldest; babysits for the Scanlons; friends with Sophie and Sarah Martin
  - **Nicole Nash** – Loretta and Paul Martin's daughter; kidney recipient from Susan Scanlon
  - **Sean Nash** – Loretta's son; apprentice to David Wheeler at Forever Friends and Westbury Animal Hospital
  - **Frank Haynes** – Westbury town councilmember; business owner; founder of Forever Friends dog rescue; married to Loretta; grandson of Hector Martin; father of twins Bonnie and Branson
  - **Bonnie and Branson Haynes** – twins of Frank and Loretta

- **Ingrid** – Haynes family nanny; former pediatric ICU nurse

· *The Wheelers*

- **David Wheeler** – works with therapy dogs; helps at Forever Friends and Westbury Animal Hospital; Grace Acosta's boyfriend; son of William and Jackie Wheeler
- **Jackie Wheeler** – wife of disgraced mayor William Wheeler; mother of David
- **William Wheeler (deceased)** – disgraced former mayor; convicted of fraud and embezzlement; died in prison

· *Friends, Neighbors and Westbury Community*

- **Anita Archer** – owner of Archer's Bridal
- **Gordon Mortimer** – antiques dealer/appraiser; Anita's love interest
- **Judy Young (née Jorgenson)** – owner of Celebrations Gift Shop; town gossip and Maggie's loyal friend; wife of Jeff
- **Jeff Carson** — uncle owned the Olsson House; married to Judy
- **Sunday Sloan** – rare-book librarian at Highpointe College; Josh Newlon's love interest
- **Josh Newlon** – Maggie's assistant; son of Lyla Kershaw; in a relationship with Sunday
- **Lyla Kershaw** – Josh's birth mother; works in accounting at Highpointe College library; Sunday's close friend
- **Charlotte** – owner of Candy Alley candy shop

- **Laura and Pete Fitzpatrick** – Laura owns the bakery; Pete owns Pete's Bistro, local hotspot for town leaders; one child
- **Harriet and Larry Burman** – owners of Burman Jewelers
- **Joan and Sam Torres** – Maggie's first friends in Westbury; Joan is a police dispatcher, Sam a handyman
- **Tim Knudsen** – realtor; town councilmember; married to Nancy; grandfather to Zack
- **Gloria Harper Vaughn and Glenn Vaughn** – married; residents of Fairview Terraces; surrogate grandparents to David Wheeler
- **Chief Andy Thomas** – Westbury police chief
- **George and Tonya Holmes** – married with three children; Tonya is a councilmember and Maggie's friend
- **Louise** – workroom supervisor at Archer's Bridal
- **Dolores** – seamstress at Archer's Bridal

· ***Highpointe College and Beyond***

- **Dr. Fiona Locke** – Dean of Highpointe College Geology Department
- **Colleen Connelly** – Maggie's Administrative Assistant, replacing Josh Newlon
- **Robert Harris** – rare-book librarian at Cambridge University; friend to Sunday; biological father of Josh
- **Anthony Plume** – dean of Hightpointe College English Department; rare-book thief; ally of Nigel Blythe
- **Nigel Blythe** – London rare-book dealer;

poisoned Hazel Harrington; attempted to kill Sunday and Anthony

- **Hazel Harrington (deceased)** – former rare-book librarian at Highpointe College, murdered by Blythe
- **Ian Lawry** – former president of Highpointe College
- **Russell Isaac** – auto-parts heir; former acting mayor; involved in embezzlement scheme with Delgados
- **Forest Smith (deceased)** – attorney; died in suspicious fall off bridge
- **Bill Stetson** – attorney at Stetson & Graham
- **Yolanda and Malcolm Yates** – Malcolm, college president and late Paul Martin's colleague; Yolanda, his wife

- ***Other Notables***
- **Delgado Brothers** – embezzlers of town pension fund
- **Chuck Delgado** – former councilmember; liquor store owner
- **Ron** – CPA and investment advisor; married to William Wheeler's sister
- **Mary** – single mother; administrative assistant at Haynes Enterprises
- **Juan** – vet tech at Westbury Animal Hospital
- **Sherry and Neil Parker** – Sherry is new vet at Westbury Animal Hospital; Neil now runs Haynes Enterprises
- **Jack Rodriguez** – David's landlord in California

- **Lyndon Upton** – professor of finance, University of Chicago; Maggie's former colleague
- **Pam Olson and Steve Turner** – Maggie and John's friends from New England and hosts of the home-improvement TV show *Wishes of Home*

RECURRING PETS

Rosemont Series Recurring Pets

Blossom, Buttercup, and Bubbles—Maggie and John's kittens, named after PowerPuff Girls

Cara—small female German Shepherd adopted by Josh Newlon. Black with a caramel-colored face

Cooper—Susan and Aaron Scanlon's dog, a gift from David Wheeler. A young Golden Retriever who is calm and gentle with baby Julia

Daisy—Nash children's dog, an Aussie/cattle dog mix female

Dan—Josh Newlon's dog, huge black lab, has calming effect on baby Julia

Dodger—David Wheeler's dog, mid-sized mutt with one eye. Therapy dog

Dory—Jack Rodriguez's Westie

Eve—shows up at Rosemont on Maggie's first night, stray, small female terrier mix

Magellan—Tommy Acosta's cat

Namor—David Wheeler's cat whose name is Roman spelled backward, gray with 4 white paws

Roman—John Allen's dog, gentle Golden Retriever

Rusty—Sam and Joan Torres's dog

Sally—Frank Haynes' dog, overweight border collie mix

Snowball—Nash children's dog, a terrier/schnauzer mix male

Sparky—Tim Knudsen's grandson's dog/medium-sized crossbreed with curly brown and white coat

ABOUT THE AUTHOR

USA Today Bestselling Author BARBARA HINSKE is an attorney and novelist. She's authored the Guiding Emily series, the mystery thriller collection "Who's There?", the Paws & Pastries series, three novellas in The Wishing Tree series, and the beloved *Rosemont Series. Guiding Emily* was made into a Hallmark Channel movie of the same name in 2023 and her novella *The Christmas Club* was made into a Hallmark Channel movie of the same name in 2019.

She is extremely grateful to her readers! She inherited the writing gene from her father who wrote mysteries when he retired and told her a story every night of her childhood. She and her husband share their own Rosemont with two adorable and spoiled dogs. The old house keeps her husband busy with repair projects and her happily decorating, entertaining, and gardening. She also spends a lot of time baking and—as a result—dieting.

ALSO BY BARBARA HINSKE

Available at Amazon in Print, Audio, and for Kindle

The Rosemont Series

Coming to Rosemont

Weaving the Strands

Uncovering Secrets

Drawing Close

Bringing Them Home

Shelving Doubts

Restoring What Was Lost

No Matter How Far

When Dreams There Be

Waves of Grace

Threads of Kindness

Love and Legacy

Novellas

The Night Train

The Christmas Club (adapted

for The Hallmark Channel, 2019)

Paws & Pastries

Sweets & Treats

Snowflakes, Cupcakes & Kittens

Tarts & Turnovers

Pies & Plans

Workout Wishes & Valentine Kisses

Wishes of Home

Wishful Tails

Back in the Pack

Novels in the Guiding Emily Series

Guiding Emily (adapted for The Hallmark Channel, 2023)

The Unexpected Path

Over Every Hurdle

Down the Aisle

From the Heart

Growing the Circle

Novels in the "Who's There?!" Collection

Deadly Parcel

Final Circuit

CONNECT WITH BARBARA HINSKE

Sign up for her newsletter at **BarbaraHinske.com**

Goodreads.com/BarbaraHinske

Facebook.com/BHinske

Instagram/barbarahinskeauthor

Pinterest.com/BarbaraHinske

BookBub/Barbara Hinske

Twitter(X)/Barbara Hinske

TikTok.com/BarbaraHinske

Search for **Barbara Hinske on YouTub**e

bhinske@gmail.com